SPINE TINGLERS

Published by
ROTHCO PRESS
1331 Havenhurst Drive #103
West Hollywood, CA 90046

Cover Design: Rob Cohen
Illustration Design with Adobe Firefly

Rothco Press is a division of Over Easy Media Inc.
www.RothcoPress.com
@RothcoPress

Spine Tinglers
Paperback - 978-1-945436-37-6

SPINE TINGLERS

Lisa Morton

ROTHCO PRESS • LOS ANGELES, CALIFORNIA

Table of Contents

INTRODUCTION:

Back around five years ago, I started working with producers Rob Cohen and Christine Roth, when they inaugurated the podcast *Ghost Magnet With Bridget Marquardt* and invited me to tag along to provide the weekly "Ghost Report." I'd known Rob and Christine for a few years already, and we'd talked about doing a variety of different things, including a weekly horror fiction podcast.

Not long after *Ghost Magnet* started streaming, we got more serious about that fiction idea. I've been writing and publishing horror short stories since 1993 (my first sale, "Sane Reaction," was based on a one-act play I'd written and directed, and the story version appeared in the British paperback Dark Voices 6). Since that initial sale, I'd written and sold many more short stories (even winning the prestigious Bram Stoker Award for one), and had become skilled at writing them quickly. This is why the idea of a weekly fiction podcast didn't completely terrify me; as long as the stories were kept fairly short – no more than 1,000-1,500 words (or 10-15 minutes to read out loud) – I felt fairly sure I could keep up with the schedule, even while I was writing other things.

Well, I not only kept up with it, I ended up enjoying the heck out of it. Sometimes I'd end a long day of work by going into my backyard with something to sip, sitting down, and just writing. It was sheer bliss! I've never suffered from any short-age of ideas (I think one of the most common misconceptions among non-writers is that ideas are hard to come by – sorry, they're not; it's the time to sit down and write them that can be the most difficult aspect of writing). Sometimes I'd know what I wanted to write about when I sat down; other times, I'd just look around and let inspiration strike. That weird hum in the air? "The Hum." The poppies that had sprung up in my yard after an early spring rain? "Poppies." That dog next door that wouldn't stop barking? "Bruno."

The stories piled up quickly. We came up with our title, *Spine Tinglers*, and it was time for producers Rob and Christine to take over. They'd always envisioned Spine Tinglers as having a differ-ent reader every week, someone who was a celebrity in paranor-mal or entertainment circles. Sometimes they'd give me the name of a person they had access to, and I'd write a story specifically for that reader (i.e., "The Psychic" or "Renfield's Revenge").

Unfortunately, finding and recording those readers proved to be a lot tougher than writing the stories. We recorded less than a dozen before we all moved onto other projects and the Spine Tinglers podcast just kind of evaporated.

Except…I'd written 35 stories specifically for Spine Tinglers.

As we neared the end of 2023, we talked about resurrecting Spine Tinglers, albeit transmogrified – it would be reborn as a book, with hopes of eventually getting the podcast going again.

And so, here it is, many years after the idea was born…*Spine Tinglers* the book.

I certainly enjoyed writing these little offerings, and I hope you'll enjoy reading (or maybe listening!) to them.

Is your spine ready?

THE BASEMENT

Alex stood on the landing, looking down at the dimly-lit staircase. He hated having to go down into the basement. Of course no one who worked at JT's Liquor wanted to go down there; the space was inexplicably huge, with side-rooms and alcoves that were unlit. Except for a few of the better bottles of wine that JT kept down here, the basement had been unused for decades. It was impossible now to guess what it had once been used for. Alex's co-worker Derren liked to joke that it had obviously been designed to hold satanic rituals in.

Even just going down there was an unhappy adventure. The stairs were ancient, rotting timber that creaked and felt suspiciously loose in places; they were narrow and gloomy, with a hard, dirty concrete floor waiting at the bottom. JT kept saying he'd look into replacing the old wood, but in the meantime Alex always held his breath whenever he got sent down to retrieve a rare bottle of cabernet for a wealthy customer.

It was January, and even in Los Angeles that meant it was cold and damp. Alex felt the temperature drop as he made his way down the stairs; he was shivering by the time he reached the bottom.

It was also completely dark. Anxious and chilled, his fingers crawled the cracking wall until he found the light-switch. The single bulb overhead went on, illuminating the waist-high wine rack in the center of the huge room.

He tried to focus on the task of finding the specific bottle, not looking around at the maze of cobwebbed rooms. Shapes loomed just inside doors; sounds echoed eerily through the space. Some of the sounds came from below.

Kneeling before the rack, Alex pulled out bottles, checking labels before sliding them back into their spots. He kept meaning to come down here and organize the bottles, but it was one more task that never got done because it involved the basement.

Alex suddenly trembled, realizing it felt like the temperature had just dropped even more. He could see his breath now in the lone lamp. The atmosphere in the room felt heavy, as if he was at the bottom of the sea. He tried to push aside his growing unease. Where was that bottle?

He made the mistake then of glancing up, and saw something that froze his heart: the air thirty feet away was moving, a dim shape that rose as Alex did. He forgot the bottle as he watched something take form in the unlit room across from him. It moved when he did, and he found himself drawn towards it. Even as his mind screamed at him to flee, his feet pulled him toward the amorphous, glowing shape.

When he was two feet from it, gripped by both terror and curiosity, he raised an arm to reach out – and his fingers encountered something solid, flat, glassy…

A mirror.

The ghostly shape was in the mirror. Which could only mean –

Alex spun and saw a body splayed out on the filthy floor at the bottom of the steps. His own dead eyes stared up at him, and he realized that he hadn't survived this trip down those stairs that JT really should have replaced.

His scream was silent as he realized where he'd be spending eternity.

BRUNO

As the doctor unwrapped Tessa's right index finger, she felt hope give way to despair.

It was a full inch shorter than her other fingers. Dr. Abramson saw her dismay and tried to sound compassionate. "I'm sorry," she said, "there was just too much damage to save the whole finger."

Knowing it was stupid even as the words came out of her mouth, Tessa asked, "And it won't grow back?"

Tessa's mom put a sympathetic hand on her back. "I'm afraid not," said Dr. Abramson. "But at least the other injuries from the attack were minor and shouldn't leave any scars."

The attack…

"I hate that dog," Tessa whispered.

"So do I, honey," Mom said. "Now let's go home."

Tessa saw the dog every morning on her way to Alexander Hamilton High. His name was Bruno, and he was a huge German Shepherd owned by a thirtysomething muscleman with a shaven head and a lot of tattoos that Tessa thought were probably gang signs. His house was right in the narrowest part of the street, between her home and her school. It was only three blocks to her school, but since the attack Tessa's mom had driven her every day.

Usually Bruno was kept in his fenced-in front yard. Tessa still passed that yard on the far side of the street; anyone who had the audacity of walking on the public sidewalk in front of Bruno's yard was subjected to a heart-stopping display of vicious barking as the dog hurled his bulk against the fence over and over. Bruno's owner had acquired him two years ago; Tessa had walked by him almost every day since, so she'd gotten used to the uproar. Even walking on the far side of the street drove the dog to hysterics.

But a week ago, Tessa had been passing the house on her way to school in the morning when she hadn't heard anything…at least not at first. She'd actually slowed down, sensing that something was wrong. Suddenly Bruno had charged her from behind a nearby parked car, still trailing a length of chain that had somehow snapped. Tessa had run, but Bruno was faster; he'd leapt onto her from behind. Fortunately her backpack had shielded her from the worst of it, but when she'd instinctively held up a hand, Bruno had bitten off part of the index finger. Just then she'd heard shouting and Bruno's owner had run up, grabbing the chain and pulling the dog away. As Tessa sat up, covered in bruises and blood, she'd seen the man walking away, dragging Bruno. "Your dog just attacked me!" she yelled after him.

"You shouldn't be walking in this neighborhood," the man shouted back without even turning.

Tessa had limped back home. Fortunately her mom hadn't left for work yet, so she called in and then rushed Tessa to the hospital. They'd cleaned the wounds, given Tessa as much comfort as a bureaucracy was allowed to, handed over the large bill, and sent them home.

Tessa had wanted to be a pianist. She was good; she played in all the school shows. Her mother had hopes that her musical skills would land her a scholarship; Tessa wanted to play in an all-girl rock band.

Now she couldn't reach the most important keys.

The doctors said that she should be able to re-learn how to play, but Tessa had her doubts. The entire balance of her hand had been changed.

Bruno had taken more – *much* more – than just part of her finger.

Of course Mom had gone ballistic on the owner, screaming at him through the fence around the yard, but he hadn't come out. She started looking for an attorney.

Two days after the doctor had unwrapped her mutilated finger, Tessa heard at school that Bruno was found dead in the yard. At first she didn't believe it…but when she walked home from school that afternoon, there was no frantic barking, no thuds as the fence shook.

It was true – Bruno was gone.

Tessa wondered if her Mom had done it. Or maybe it was Derren at school, who liked her and was the one who'd told her about Bruno. Heck, it was likeliest to have been one of the neighbors; she wasn't the only kid Bruno had ever attacked.

The next morning Tessa awoke to a gray, cold, early winter day. She put on a heavy sweater, scarf, and mittens that she also liked because they hid her gnawed finger. It wasn't raining, but a heavy mist hung low over everything. She could barely see fifty feet in front of her.

As she approached Bruno's yard she started to cross the street – then caught herself. *If Bruno's really gone, I don't have to…if he's gone.* She forced herself to stay on this side, trembling as she approached the beginning of the chain-link fence.

There was no sign of Bruno.

It's true – he's gone. Tessa was just feeling some weight lift from her when she heard it: paws running on grass, and a frantic barking that sounded like it came from the far end of a long tunnel. Skin crawling, she tried to peer through the mist.

He's not dead.

But something was wrong; there was no sign of Bruno, even through the haze. And the sound…it wasn't right. A word popped into Tessa's head:

Ghost.

She knew then: the dog had died, but its fury hadn't. It would patrol this yard, maybe forever.

Realizing that, she felt pity for the animal. "I'm sorry," she whispered through the fence, before adding, "but you can't hurt me anymore."

The barking stopped.

Tessa continued onto school, knowing that she'd never have to walk on the far side of the street again.

THE INVESTIGATION

The *Maximum Ghosts* podcast team arrived at Marston State Lunatic Asylum at just after 9 p.m. on a Friday night. Normally Lindsey would never have referred to any institution as a "lunatic asylum", but that was actually how the ancient wooden sign before the huge old structure read.

"Look at this place," Jay said, eyeing the three-story brick building as he lugged a duffel bag of cameras, mics, tablets, and laptops.

Kenzie, their medium, shivered even though it was late July and still 80 degrees at night. "The vibes are already crazy and we're not even inside yet."

Lindsey had paid well to reserve the historic site for her team of four for the entire weekend, hoping that one more boost in their YouTube numbers might lead to a television deal. There were nibbles already; one spectacular EVP or – even better – a full-body apparition and they might never have to worry about day jobs ever again.

An hour later, they'd chosen the former day room on the second floor and set up their base camp there. In the past, this floor had also housed the mens' dormitory, bathrooms and shower rooms, treatment rooms, and a few doctors' offices. Marston had been shut down as a working institution in 1968, and it had already been edging toward ruin then; although it had served briefly as a jail in the '70s and a haunted attraction in the 2000s, it had been accumulating dust, cobwebs, and rot for half-a-century.

"Tell me again," said Brian, their main techie, "what we're looking for."

Lindsey brought up the file on her phone, swiping through her research. "There've been four main ghosts reported here: one is a little boy who is mainly seen on the first floor; one is a patient named Darby who is supposed to be helpful; one's a shadow figure on this floor; and the scariest is supposed to be a patient named Arch who has been known to punch or scratch."

Jay wandered the unlit day room, a flashlight in one hand and a K-II meter in the other. The day room held a cracked leather couch that no amount of money could've gotten Lindsey to sit on, the splintered remains of some tables and cheers, several windows still barred, pools of moldy water in the corners, and a lot of graffiti on the walls.

"Getting anything?" Lindsey asked.

Jay stared intently at the meter. "Yeah, there's definitely some activity in here –"

He broke off as Kenzie gasped loudly and blurted out, "Something's here…"

Lindsey motioned Brian forward with a digital thermometer before asking, "Do you know who?"

Closing her eyes, Kenzie answered, "I think…it's a young man…"

Brian looked up at Lindsey, eyes wide, and waved the thermometer at her – but she didn't need to see the glowing numbers to feel the chill surrounding the medium.

Kenzie smiled, and opened her eyes. "Darby's here. And they're right – he's a sweetheart."

Lindsey inwardly cursed as she realized they didn't have a camera on Kenzie, but then Jay ran up, phone held out before him. "Does Darby have a message for us?"

Kenzie's eyes lost their focus. "He's just…"

A chair on the other side of the room flipped completely over.

The four investigators froze in shock for a second, then Brian whispered to Lindsay, "We got that on audio, at least."

"Darby," Lindsey asked, "did you do that?"

A dark figure moved across the doorway behind Kenzie. *Shadow figure…?*

"They're *all* here," Kenzie said, as she clutched herself, shaking.

Now they all felt it. Lindsey wasn't a sensitive and rarely experienced the atmospheric changes that Kenzie reported, but this time it was undeniable: the air felt dense, pressurized, weighing down on them. Brian began to pant. Jay frowned as he asked, "If they're all here…does that mean Arch, too?"

Arch…the one who hurt people.

"Yes, but…" Kenzie hesitated before adding, "Darby is holding him back so we're safe."

Lindsey didn't feel safe; in fact, she'd never wanted to run screaming from one of their investigations before. "Kenzie," she asked, "can you get more information about Arch – maybe a full name, when he was here, what his diagnosis was, anything?"

"His name…the last name was something like Doran, Duran…no – *Dursler*."

Lindsey had access to the entire history of Marston, and she searched the records now. There it was: *Dursler, Archibald*. As she opened the file, Brian said, "You know what? It's dropped thirty degrees in here, the K-II is off the charts, and…I'm sorry, but I think we should go."

"No," Kenzie said, "we're okay – Darby says we're fine."

Lindsey read through Dursler's file. He'd been sent to Marston in 1927 after going on a murder spree, killing six people with a knife. He'd spent thirty years in Marston, often in restraints, before dying in 1957. Then Lindsey saw something that made her stuff her phone in a pocket and call out to her team, "We're getting out of here now."

Jay, always the most fearless one, asked, "Why?"

"Because Archibald Dursler suffered from multiple personalities – one of whom was named Darby. We've been seriously *had*."

Kenzie screamed then as the first scratch appeared across her throat. From somewhere in the depths of the Marston Asylum, Lindsey felt something powerful laughing at them as it unleashed.

INCIDENT IN A DRUGSTORE PARKING LOT

"That'll be $2.76," says the vampire behind the drugstore counter.

As I dig the money out of my wallet, I swear I can feel his eyes on my neck. He's a kid, barely legal, was probably a college junior or senior before the wars. I would think, *Poor kid*, but, after all, he'd rip my throat out and drink my blood if he thought he could get away with it.

I hand him the bills. It's after midnight, and I don't see anyone else in the store. As the kid counts out my change, I see the tips of his fangs poking out over his lower lip.

"Do you need a bag?" he asks.

I tell him I don't, pick up my soda and candy bar, and head for the exit.

The parking lot outside is empty. I'm not sure why I parked so far from the entrance to the drugstore, the only 24-hour business in this block.

While I cross to my car, un-wrapping the candy bar, I give in to anger over the kid and his situation. When the vampires started to appear three years ago, that boy was probably like me: laughing at the early reports, and then panicking as we realized it was real, that there really were monsters out there who had returned from the grave to suck the blood of the living after the sun went down. They were incredibly strong and everyone they bit also turned and they could only be killed by wooden stakes through the heart, but in most respects they weren't anything like the old movies and books – they couldn't turn into bats or mist, they weren't afraid of crucifixes, and they weren't driven only by bloodlust. They were more like desperate people who had a weird disease.

But war broke out anyways, a war that ended only with the Treaty of '26: the vampires and humans would no longer hunt and kill each other, as long as every able-bodied human donated blood once every two months and the vampires lived on that. It had worked out just fine: humans liked the extra money the government gave them for the blood, and the vampires turned out to be cheap labor for the late-night jobs that nobody else wanted to do. When the kid in the drugstore got off work just before the sun rose, he'd probably go home to his cheap apartment with the blackout paper taped over the windows, play a video game until he fell asleep in his futon, maybe sext his vamp girlfriend.

I was thinking about all that as I chewed my candy bar and was halfway to my car when I heard the voice behind me: "Excuse me…"

It was the kid, following me out of the drugstore, across the empty parking lot.

I'd heard the rumors about this kind of stuff, just like everyone else had – the rogue vampire killings that got hushed up, the ones where they lured some idiot by getting them alone somewhere, getting them to turn around so they could launch themselves at your throat –

I wasn't about to turn around. Instead, I walked faster.

"Uh, hello – excuse me, your wallet –"

I was almost at my car. Just a few more yards. How close was he? I could hear his footsteps on the asphalt, getting closer and closer…

Heart hammering, I walked faster. I almost ran, but I was nearly at the car. I threw the candy wrapper aside and pulled out my keys. I punched the button that would open the trunk.

"You left your wallet –"

The trunk lid popped up. I tossed the can of soda in, and grabbed the crossbow in there, spinning now to face the kid.

I forced myself not to fire right away. I wanted to savor the look on his face for a second, the shock that spread across his pale features as he saw what I had and knew what I was about to do with it.

"No, c'mon, hold on –"

I fired. All the practice with the crossbow had paid off; the arrow went straight into his heart. He was dead before he hit the pavement.

I returned the crossbow to the trunk, closed the lid, and then went over to get the wallet I'd deliberately left on the counter. The bolt stuck straight up out of his chest, the six black stripes on it visible even in the sodium lights. They'd find it in the morning, just like they'd find the other 150 vamps that other members of our militia had killed tonight with similarly-marked arrows and stakes and bolts, and they'd know that some of us were done donating blood six times a year just to keep these assholes alive. We're reclaiming our rights to our own blood.

Look out, bloodsuckers – the war is back on.

THE BOOKSTORE

Jake stood outside the abandoned single-story building, with its overgrown and cracked parking lot, boarded-over windows and sagging roof, feeling a tug inside. He took another pull from the tequila bottle even though he was already staggering.

"See, bro?" his bandmate Casper said, nodding at the boarded-over windows.

Squinting through the gloom of the poorly-lit and desolate urban street, Jake made out the chipped and faded lettering over the doorway. "'Book Heaven'," he murmured. "It sure was. I've got so many memories of this place…"

His girlfriend Amanda took the tequila bottle from him, gulped down a double-shot, and entwined herself around him. "Sorry, baby, but it looks more like Book Hell now."

Jake's voice caught as he answered, "It was the greatest place on earth. Aisle after aisle of dusty, used books, everything you could've wanted, all of it priced cheap enough to be affordable on a ten-year-old's allowance.

"That must've been right before it closed," Casper said. "It's been locked up since '95."

"Why haven't they sold the building?" Amanda asked.

Grinning, Casper said, "They can't. Everybody they've showed it to got freaked out. They say it's haunted. Heck, the old dude who owned it just corked right there in the store. They'll probably just demolish it one of these days."

Jake's palms itched as he thought about those days of rummaging through the stacks, finding paperback Clive Barker books for a buck, that scaryass one about the investigation team in the Belasco house, the Stephen King book with the all-black cover except for the one drop of blood… "Wonder what happened to the stock?"

Casper shrugged. "Maybe it's still in there."

Jake turned to look at Amanda, who smiled at him expectantly, instantly boosting his courage. "That's it – we gotta get in there."

Casper reached under his leather jacket and pulled a crowbar out from beneath it. "I thought you might say that."

"Are you serious, man?"

Waving at the mostly-abandoned shops, Casper answered, "You see anybody around here who's gonna care? C'mon." He started walking forward. Jake glanced at Amanda, who pulled him along. "It'll be fun," she said.

The front of the store was covered by a rolling metal grill, secured by a padlock through a chain. All of it was old and rusted, and by the time Jake and Amanda reached it, Casper had snapped the padlock, flung the chain aside, and was struggling to roll back the grill. "Gimme a hand here…"

The corroded iron shrieked in protest as they pushed it back enough to expose the splintered wood door. Jake looked back nervously, but nobody was coming; this late at night, there wasn't even traffic on the street. One yank of the crowbar on the moldering doorframe, and the door swung out. Casper pulled it back, the hinges sounding like a bad sound effect, bowing to Jake. "Your kingdom awaits."

Heart hammering, Jake pulled out his phone, set it to flashlight mode, and stepped in, Amanda and Casper following.

It took him a few seconds to make the dusty, cobwebbed mess he was seeing match up with his memories of spending idyllic afternoons here, scouring the shelves for horror novels he hadn't read while Mom browsed the Romance section. There were books still here – a lot of them – but those on the bottom shelves had been chewed by rats and silverfish, while the ones higher up were so mounded with dust that their titles were unreadable.

Jake didn't have to read those titles, though; he could've found the Horror area blindfolded. He stepped around the remains of a squatter's fire ("Not a reader, I guess," Amanda commented, noting burned pages) as he headed for the back of the store. He stepped around one tall bookcase – and stopped, frozen, as he saw two glowing eyes peering at him twenty feet away. Then he realized: his phone light had caught an old paperback cover. Eyes had been big in the '80s.

"Whoa," Casper said from somewhere nearby, "This place stinks like an outhouse. I think somebody lived in here."

Jake paid him no attention, because he'd reached the Horror section. Joy and wonder and remembered terrors on summer afternoons rose up before him. Gasping, he began pulling old paperbacks from the shelves, blowing dust off to read the titles and authors. "Holy crap," he blurted out, "here's *The Light at the End* by Skipp and Spector! *The Woods are Dark* by Richard Laymon! And, oh my God – *Halloween II* by Jack Martin!"

"You really love this stuff, don't you, baby?" Amanda asked as she pressed herself against him.

"I sure do —" Jake broke off in shock as he glanced at Amanda, and saw that her face had changed into that of a scheming, seductive succubus, her jeans and band t-shirt replaced with a flowing white gown. It took Jake a second to realize that she looked like the sexy yet terrifying women that had graced so many of those paperback covers.

He blinked, and normal Amanda was back, peering at him curiously. "You okay?"

Shaking it off, Jake nodded. "Yeah…that was…I guess I had too much to drink or something –"

Casper screamed.

They couldn't see him, but both Jake and Amanda instinctively called their friend's name and rushed toward the sound. They rounded a corner, brushing aside cobwebs, and saw Casper prone, with what looked like a small boy bent over him. As Jake's light caught the boy, he turned to look up at them, revealing a grinning skull in place of a head. There was blood on the boy-thing's hands, blood that had come from Casper's torn neck.

Amanda half-shrieked and staggered away. "Let's get out of here!" She started to run toward the front door, but paused when she realized Jake wasn't following.

"Go outside and call 911! I'll be right there."

As Amanda fled, Jake looked down at the skeletal little demon before him, feeling not fear, but warm recognition. He knew this creature…he'd seen it on book covers. It nodded to him, and glanced back. Jake followed the look to see another bony thing step out of the shadows, this one dressed like a cheerleader. It approached slowly, respectfully, and then extended a hand.

Jake hesitated, knowing somehow that if he took that hand he'd be trapped here forever, with all of the books he'd grown up loving, books that had somehow become the real ghosts haunting this place, and that now invited him to join them. He sensed them waiting, inviting…

He reached out for the hand.

JAM

"*Aww, nooo…*" Tommy mutters as he sees stopped taillights on the freeway in front of him.

He slams on the brakes – he's been doing 85, and those lights are coming up really fast. The car fishtails slightly and Tommy laughs. Usually he gets paid for doing this.

He's got a gig tonight for a night shoot; it's an action movie about an everyday cop chasing a rogue Federal agent, and they called Tommy to double the cop in a car roll-over stunt. Tommy's call time is midnight. It's 11:40 p.m. now.

"Damn it," he says, as the car comes to a dead stop.

The entire freeway is frozen on both sides. Tommy hasn't seen any construction alerts, so he figures it's either one whopping big accident or maybe police cornering a carjacking suspect.

He's been in his motionless car for all of fifteen seconds before he starts to get anxious. He could probably still make it on time if he can get off the freeway, but he's now blocked in on all sides. He's got no choice but to sit this out.

A minute passes, as he drums his fingers to hiphop music, then he rolls his window down and cranes his neck out, trying to get a view of what's ahead. He can't really see more than a few cars in front of him, but then he spots something that makes him stare: a car two in front of him has its doors open.

What...?

Curious now, Tommy looks around, sees the traffic is unlikely to start moving, and he undoes his seatbelt. He opens his door and steps out to get a better view. That car, a black SUV, has the driver's side door just hanging open.

A horn behind Tommy honks, startling him. It's the driver of the car behind him, warning him to get back in his car. Tommy ignores it to walk forward. He's focused on the open door. "Hello?" he calls out.

He sees something under the open car door – feet. On the asphalt. A dark pool is forming around them.

A chill runs through Tommy. He's about to go check on the body when something crunches underfoot – glass. He looks down and sees the driver's side window of the car directly in front of his is smashed. The driver is still behind the wheel but sitting in a strange position, her head, back, mouth open –

Looking more closely, Tommy sees her glassy eyes, the blood staining the front of her blouse.

His adrenaline kicking in, Tommy runs back to his own car, but stops when he hears something, coming from ahead of him: it's a roaring sound, like a hundred lions in a wind tunnel. Then he sees *something* – or rather, he sees the absence of something, because there's a moving black shape blotting out the lights of the cars and the freeway. The black shape is tall, maybe seven feet, moving between the cars, then leaping up to a roof. As Tommy watches, the living void smashes another window; there's a scream from within the car, then the driver is pulled halfway out of the vehicle and blood from his throat suddenly fountains, splattering the nearest cars. Tommy watches until the shape finishes shaking the life out of its victim. It turns his way.

He runs, his trapped car forgotten. He races through the stopped cars, heading for an exit ramp a half-mile back. Tommy's only thought is to get off the freeway and hope this thing won't follow him, that it will continue its freeway killing spree. He's still got his phone in his pocket, so if he can get a moment to breathe –

But the thing is *fast*, and it's catching up to him. He uses his stuntman skills to leap and roll over a car, but the thing easily follows. Now it's only fifty…forty…thirty feet behind him.

He won't make the off-ramp.

But there's an overpass in front of him. He runs to it and leaps atop the waist-high barricade there. It's a long jump down to the street below. Even he can't manage that without breaking something serious. But the thing is almost behind him –

There's a truck coming, a big moving truck heading for the underpass. If he can time the leap…

His heart is hammering as he perches on the barricade. The truck is moving too slowly…

"C'mon," Tommy says between gritted teeth. The *thing* is almost on him, he can hear that awful roaring sound right behind him –

He jumps.

He lands on the truck roof and rolls, just like he's done a dozen times on film. He almost rolls too far, but manages to stop just as he reaches the edge. His fingers instinctively reach out and clutch the metal side of the truck.

He made it.

Then the truck's brakes shriek and it begins to jack-knife. As the truck slams into another of the formless, colorless things, Tommy realizes that he's going to be very late to work.

THE GARGOYLE

Amber walked up to the office building at exactly 8:20 a.m., the way she did every weekday. After being awoken by her alarm clock at 6:45, she'd left the house at 7:30, fought the morning traffic for forty minutes, arrived at the garage and parked, and was now about to take the elevator up to the ninth floor to begin her job as receptionist at the firm of Chambers & Bierce. There had been absolutely nothing unusual about her day so far.

Nothing, that is, until the moment when she was about to pass through the main entrance into the lobby, but some instinct told her to look up.

She paused on the sidewalk before the Hamilton Building. Built in 1898, the imposing stone structure had been a ten-floor marvel at the time, and it had survived with few changes since.

Amber looked up, seeing the gray blocks, the windows, the ornamentation –

The *gargoyles*. The Hamilton was ringed with them just above the second floor. There were three to a side, each one a different, leering demon. Amber had heard that the sculptor had copied the famed gargoyles of Notre Dame, but she'd never bothered to look that up. The one directly overhead was the eeriest; with tall horns, half-lidded eyes, and a fanged grin, crouching, gripping the ledge with knife-like claws, it looked like something straight out of *Dante's Inferno*.

As Amber eyed the awful thing, a chill of recognition raced through her: she'd dreamed about it. Last night, at 3 a.m., she'd awakened gasping, remembering a dream of the leering stone demon turning to look at her.

Now, five hours later, she stood there waiting, heart racing, expecting the head to slowly turn…

Nothing happened.

Of course, Amber thought to herself. *Silly…it was just a bad dream is all. Who wouldn't have a bad dream about that thing?*

She imagined flipping the gargoyle off and walked into the building before she was late for work.

She dreamed of the gargoyle again that night. This time, when she came up out of sleep, she remembered seeing it look at her before it stretched out great wings and launched itself from the building.

On the drive into work that morning, the news on the radio mentioned a man who'd been found murdered, torn apart, near the Hamilton Building. The crime had occurred sometime around 3 a.m. There were as yet no suspects.

Amber arrived, parked, and walked to the building, her eyes riveted the whole time on the gargoyle. She paused beneath it, looking up. What was that dark splotch on the stone around it? Had that been there yesterday?

You're being ridiculous, she chided herself.

The dreams continued every night, ten nights in a row. In the last one she saw the gargoyle chewing on a human arm, the fingers dangling over the side of the ledge.

The news reported new victims found in the downtown area.

On the eleventh morning, she paused beneath the gargoyle, looking up – and something warm and thick fell onto her forehead.

She reached up, swiped at the spot, looked at her fingers. They were smeared red. When she looked up again, she saw blood plainly dripping off the ledge around the gargoyle.

Was its position just slightly different, the head angled a tiny bit lower, the claws a few inches to the left of where they had been?

Amber decided it was time to call the police. She wouldn't tell them about her dreams, only that there was blood dripping from the ledge. They connected her with a homicide detective in charge of what was now called "the Downtown Ripper Case". He listened as she described the blood; he asked her why she thought it was connected to the murders. She stuttered through some explanation about the building's proximity to the murders that she wasn't sure the detective believed.

But that afternoon, he showed up to interview her in person. They had found blood on the ledge. It matched that of the last victim.

Amber had a hard time getting to sleep that night. She didn't want to see the gargoyle again, didn't want to awaken with a jolt and a memory of seeing it doing something terrible. But finally she drifted off just after 1 a.m.

When she bolted up out of bed at the same time – 3 a.m. – she remembered all too clearly: in the dream, the gargoyle had flung itself from the side of the building and was diving straight towards her.

That was when she turned and saw it sitting outside her window, grinning.

THE SKIN I'M IN

My name is Green Jordan. I'm 24 years old, I live in a studio apartment in downtown Los Angeles, I'm a personal assistant to a moderately famous artist, and I'm nonbinary.

Oh, and I'm also a werewolf.

Before you go thinking that's some kind of curse or something...it's not. I've been a werewolf for three years, ever since I got bitten leaving a club in Hollywood late one moonlit night. Once a month, on the night of the full moon, I transform, but not into some monster that walks on two legs; no, I go *wolf*-wolf, down on all fours, the whole thing.

And I *love* it. When I'm wolf, I'm sleek and powerful; when I'm wolf, nobody asks me if I'm a boy or a girl. Nobody cares. I'm just WOLF.

Here's how it works for me: on the night of the full moon, I find out when moonrise is, then I drive, either north to the Santa Susana hills or east to the San Gabriels. I've got a few favorite spots that are far removed from the nearest houses, where nobody will notice a car pulled off to one side of the road. I get out of the car, strip, pack my clothes in a backpack along with my car keys, and hide them under some bush or rock; then I wait for the moon. As soon as I see that glow starting on the horizon, I feel the tingles running all over. As the moon appears, I disappear...or rather, I become wolf. Then I run free through the hills, my four strong paws carrying me so much faster than my human feet ever could. Under the light of the moon I hunt - squirrels, rabbits, chipmunks. Sorry to disappoint those of you who wanted to hear about gory-movie-type human kills.

Although I'm in wolf form, I never stop being me. I think like me, I feel like me. As dawn approaches and the sky lightens, I know it's time to head back to where I've stashed my pack. I find it, I wait until the sun replaces the moon and Green Jordan's human form takes over from wolf. Sometimes there's still some blood, so I keep a towel in the backpack. I scrub off the remains of the night's meals, dress, get back in the car, and make it back to L.A. in time for work.

I feel awesome all day. Thinking about being wolf keeps me going.

For tonight's full moon, I'd chosen the hills above Fillmore, to the northwest of L.A.; they're steep, but uninhabited and they come down to acres of farmland. The hunting was always good there.

Except this time something was hunting me.

I noticed it first when I turned off the freeway and headed down one of the side roads, deserted at this time of night. There was another car behind me; it took the off-ramp when I did, drove the same route that I did. But at one point I turned right, and the other car kept going straight, so I figured it was just me being paranoid.

But then, once I'd found my spot and transformed, I was running up a stony hillside when I saw the car again, turning around, heading back. It slowed as it passed my car, and I thought it might stop...but it drove on past and was soon lost from sight.

The night scents were filling my nose, intoxicating me, making me want to revel in the sheer freedom, but I was also worried. What had that been about? Just a local, maybe, wondering what I was doing out here? Were they calling the cops even now?

I made myself wait for half-an-hour, but when nobody else showed up I moved on.

It was a glorious night in September, the air still warm, the wild things out in force. I'll spare any of you vegans the details of my feasting, but let's just say I soon forgot about my suspicions. By the time the night was beginning to fade, my belly was full, my mind at peace.

Until I got back to the bush where I'd stashed my pack, because it wasn't there.

I remembered clearly: it'd been a sagebrush, huge and thick, 200 feet from the road where my car was parked. It was the only sagebrush within ten yards. Nearby was a stand of prickly pear cactus I'd been careful to avoid.

I rooted through the sagebrush with building panic. Maybe an animal had dragged it out, a dog or a coyote...? I was about to turn when I heard a voice: "Looking for this?"

I turned to see a figure standing behind me, swinging my pack from one finger. They were like me, nonbinary, maybe a few years younger. I snarled, but they weren't frightened; in fact, they smiled.

"God, you're beautiful," they murmured, before adding, "oh, sorry, we haven't been properly introduced: my name's Morgan. I'm so pleased to meet you at last."

Curious now, I waited.

"See, I got a glimpse of you last month, when you were up in the hills above El Monte. I used binoculars to watch you change, then I got your license plate number."

I growled as I thought, *Sloppy. How could I have been so sloppy?*

"I found out where you lived, waited until the next full moon, and then followed you up here. Once you parked, I drove away because I didn't want to scare you. I just wanted to meet up with you once before the sun rises, so you can bite me."

My wolf-face must have looked surprised, because Morgan's eyebrows lifted. "Oh, c'mon, don't look so shocked. And I promise I won't be competition; just the bite, just enough to make me like you, and then you'll never see me again. I'll find my own places to hunt, I swear."

I got it, then: Morgan was like me, someone who just wanted to be themselves for one night a month, who for a few hours couldn't be judged or ridiculed, who could claim their power and strength then.

As I padded towards them, they tore off their jacket, tossed it aside, pulled their t-shirt away from their throat, and sat down on the hard ground. "It's okay if it hurts," Morgan said.

I bit.

THE UNMASKING

"C'mon, let's take off our masks."

Devin leaned forward, extending a hand towards Diana's face as if he intended to snatch her mask. She involuntarily stepped back, and she heard him laugh beneath his own face covering.

"You know you want to," he teased.

There was some truth to that – Diana *did* want to see all of his face. What she could make out of it – his smooth, dark brown skin, his mischievous eyes, the curly hair that he'd highlighted with blond – looked like the picture on the dating app, except of course he was smiling in the picture, not wearing the plain black cloth mask he had now. She'd thought he had nice lips.

She glanced around the park where they'd agreed to meet. Perched atop a cliff above the Pacific, it was mostly empty this time of night; the locals were all hunkered down in their homes eating food they'd had delivered and trying to remember what day of the week it was. But the park wasn't completely empty – there was a man jogging with his dog, there an older couple strolling along, the man's mask sagging under his nose. Diana involuntarily tugged hers (which featured a grinning mouth with long fangs) back up and said, "I do want to, but…there are other people around, and…well…"

"You're worried that I might have the virus," Devin said.

"Well…yeah."

"Do you want to see my vaccine i.d.?"

"No, I trust you, but…well, my friend Carli got a break-through case two weeks ago, and she still feels like shit."

"Would it help if I told you I just got test results back yesterday, and I'm negative?"

Diana rolled that around in her head: *but that was yesterday. How long did the results take – a day? A week? You could've gotten it since then. Or you could even just be lying to me, and you've never even been tested.* Instead, she said, "Yeah, but I haven't been tested. Aren't you worried about me?"

He gazed at her earnestly. "No. Because I think I could really like you, and that means you'd be worth the risk."

Diana had to admit that she really liked him, too. Since they'd connected on the app, they'd already exchanged texts and photos and phone calls; they'd talked about everything from what they wanted to do after graduating from college (he wanted a law degree, she wanted to travel) to their homes (he lived in an apartment with three other guys, she lived with her family) to their favorite movies (anything Marvel superhero for him, *Paranormal Activity* movies for her). They'd laughed together easily, there'd been no long, uncomfortable pauses with nothing to say.

She *did* really want to see him without a mask, and she wanted him to see her.

Just then three men rode past on bicycles. None of them wore masks, and Diana thought she heard the men say something about "idiots falling for the government's bullshit" as they pedaled away. It made the thought of removing her mask less comfortable, not more.

"Those guys are douchebags," Devin said, causing Diana to laugh. She was glad he'd said it. Once again, she realized how much she liked him.

After the cyclists left the park, Devin looked around. "Okay, so check it out: there is absolutely no one here but us now."

She followed his gaze, saw he was right; they were completely alone. To one side the park's grass and pathways meandered up to the parking lot and residential streets; on the other side, a low fence guarded against the sheer drop-off that fell fifty feet to the sea-washed rocks.

Alone.

Devin stepped slightly closer, holding out his arm. "How about this: could we just hold hands? I mean, while still keeping socially distanced?"

She nodded. She reached out and took his hand. He squeezed her fingers, rubbing them; his skin was soft and dry, and Diana felt electric sparks fly.

"See?" he said, softly, "that's not so bad."

"It's not," she agreed.

"I really want to see you," he said.

"I want to see you, too."

"What if we take off our masks, but stay six feet apart?" When Diana didn't answer, he added, "Look, if I sneeze or cough or anything, you can push me off the cliff, okay?"

Diana looked around again; the park was still empty. She released his hand and stepped away. "Okay. But you first."

He reached up and, as if performing a strip tease, slowly pulled the mask down, bit by bit, until it was completely off, dangling from his finger. Diana was pleased to see that he was as handsome as his picture. He raised his hands and his eyebrows. "So?"

"Nice," she said.

He walked up to her, slowly, teasingly, but she stood her ground, until he was just inches away. "Should I maybe take yours down with my teeth?"

Something was wrong; Diana didn't know exactly what, but she was abruptly on edge.

"Can I just give you a hug?" he asked.

Against her better judgment, she said, "Okay."

He put his arms around her, bent his head close to her ear, and whispered, "Hey, guess what?"

Diana whispered back, "What?"

"I lied…" He pulled back and coughed right into her face before saying, "I've got the virus." Then he exploded in laughter.

He howled and pointed as Diana stood, frozen. She let him continue for a few seconds; then, without another word, she reached up and began to pull her own mask down, the fabric showing a fanged smile descending to reveal –

Her own fanged smile, with teeth far longer and sharper than those printed on the mask.

Devin stopped laughing, but tried to get out one more weak chuckle. "What is that – a mask under your mask?"

"No," Diana said, striding towards him, "this is all me."

In that second Devin tried to turn and run, but her hand was on his shirt, pulling him back, slamming him to the ground. She stood over him, her huge teeth glinting wetly in the park's sodium lights.

"Look," Devin said, panicking, "it was a joke, a really bad joke, I'm sorry – I don't have the virus, okay?"

"Oh, good," Diana said, "because I didn't want to eat you if you did."

She reached down toward him, and Devin tried to pull away, shaking as he curled into a fetal position. "What are you?" he cried out.

"I'm a ghoul," Diana answered.

"A ghoul? But…ghouls only eat dead bodies, right?"

"Right…" Diana picked him up and hefted him easily over-head even as he shrieked and struggled. She walked over to the low fence bordering the cliff's edge. "…which is why I'm going to throw you over the cliff first, then feast on your dead body down below."

As Devin flew through space to crash into the rocks and pounding surf, Diana wondered how many other women he'd lied to, laughed at, treated like toys. *Oh well*, she thought, as she prepared to scramble down the cliff, *doesn't matter now.*

Because I'm hungry.

HOUSTON, WE
HAVE A PROBLEM

"Houston, we have a problem…"

Kathryn adjusted her headset, frowning. As Mission Control's CAPCOM, she'd come to know the current Space Station commander Chris Macklin well; she'd come to learn his nuances, when he was kidding and when he wasn't.

Now was one of those times he wasn't. "Roger that, Chris," she responded, as she glanced over to see Flight Director Grace Garcia waiting, "tell us what's happening."

"I'm not quite sure how to say this, but…things are floating here."

Kathryn blinked in surprise. "Say again? Floating as in…a way they're not supposed to float?"

"Roger that, Houston. Here…" Macklin made an adjustment on his end and a live camera feed appeared on one of Kathryn's monitors. It showed the interior of the International Space Station, which was a warren of narrow tubes and white walls and wires and cubicles, but floating in the center of the frame was a spacesuit, one of those used for spacewalks. "That suit," Macklin continued, "was secured in its locker five minutes ago."

"So," Kathryn asked, "why is it floating free now?"

"Because…" there was a pause before Macklin finished, "because the locker door opened by itself and this floated out."

Kathryn turned to exchange a look with Grace, who looked both concerned and slightly amused. "Sorry, Chris, but we're still not quite following…are you saying the locker door malfunctioned?"

"No. I'm saying I was looking right at it when it opened on its own. There's some other phenomena going on, too…"

"'Phenomena'?" Kathryn was glad this conversation wasn't livestreaming to the public.

"Look at this…" The view on the monitor panned jerkily away from the floating spacesuit to a laptop screen that was flickering wildly. "Have you ever seen it do that before?"

Kathryn had to admit she hadn't. Just then Grace cleared her throat and tapped her watch. Kathryn nodded before going back to the conversation with Macklin. "Chris, we're about thirty seconds out from LOS – is there anything urgent before we lose your signal?"

"Urgent? I guess not, but…well, it also feels cold in here."

Grace bent over her own monitors, checked a line, and looked back at Kathryn with a shrug. "Okay, Chris," Kathryn said, "we're going to get an EECOM to double-check that." She looked at Grace, who gave her a thumbs-up and began to speak into her own headset.

"Sounds good, Houston –" Chris's voice abruptly broke off in Kathryn's headset. There was a pause before she heard, "What the –?!" Then the loss of signal cut in and the commander's voice cut out completely.

Kathryn felt a chill of her own. Apparently she wasn't alone, because she heard Grace mutter, "What is happening up there?"

"I don't know –" Kathryn was interrupted by a burst of static in her headset. She jumped, startled; there shouldn't be any static during a regular loss of signal. But it wasn't just static; she thought she could make out a voice behind the white noise, just barely a whisper. She focused entirely on that sound, and after a few seconds she thought she could make out one word:

Komarov.

She grabbed a pad and pen, writing the word down. She continued to listen, but the voice faded away, followed by the static.

She leapt, startled again, only to realize Grace had moved up behind her and was looking down. "What's that?"

"Something I just heard in my headset."

"You couldn't have – we're in an LOS."

Kathryn tore the sheet off, staring at what she'd written. Komarov. "I know that, but…well, I heard this just now, very faint but there. It sounds familiar…"

Grace took the sheet. "It's not a word – it's a name. And it does sound familiar…"

The Flight Director returned to her own station, typing the name into a search engine. A few seconds later, she exclaimed, "Igor Komarov was a flight controller on the Russian team who died yesterday."

Andrew, the ADCO, overheard and looked up. "I knew Igor. He was a good guy, died way too young – just keeled over dead yesterday of a heart attack at 43. He was kind of bitter over the last few years, though, because he always wanted to get into space but he couldn't cut it as an astronaut. He was really envious of the spacewalks." Kathryn was surprised to see Andrew looking not anxious like everyone else in Mission Control, but pensive; then she remembered that the Attitude Determination and Control Officer was a believer in the paranormal. She'd once had a discussion with him in which he'd told her that he believed the spirit of his late grandfather lived in his house and even gave him messages. Kathryn had been slightly bewildered to square Andrew's keen engineer's mind with ghosts, but…now…

Grace said, "We've only got ten seconds now until LOS ends."

They all waited, tense – and then Chris's voice was deafening in her headset. "Houston, are you there? You're not going to believe this – hang on –"

One of the main monitors lit up with a view aboard the space station, showing Chris and the other three astronauts all suited up. "Chris," Kathryn asked, "why are you all prepped for spacewalk?"

"Because…" the camera turned from Chris and the other astronauts to the main hatch – which the empty spacesuit was now opening.

"Who's in that suit?" Grace asked.

Andrew answered, "Komarov is. He's getting his chance at space at last."

Chris's voice, panicking now, sounded in Kathryn's ear. "Houston, what the hell are we supposed to do?"

Kathryn looked around until Andrew said, "Let him go."

Without an alternative, Kathryn said, "Chris, ADCO advises to…uh…let the suit go and seal the hatch behind it."

"Roger that."

Kathryn shook as she watched the empty spacesuit unseal the hatch and step through it; it moved with strange grace, the arms and legs curving in ways that no human body could. Once it was all the way through, Chris propelled himself forward, sealing the hatch behind it.

The station's outside cameras picked up the ghost-suit moving into space. The arms waved about in a way that Kathryn almost thought was exultation; then the station moved away from it, and the suit was soon lost from view. Kathryn imagined it circling the earth a few times until it entered the atmosphere and burned up, making a shooting star that she hoped someone would see and wish on.

"He's gone," she heard Andrew murmur, "he got his wish."

Grace said, "How do we report this? I mean…did we just prove the existence of…*ghosts?*"

Kathryn saw Andrew smiling, his eyes moist, and regardless of what NASA's higher-ups decided to do with this evidence, she knew her own life would never be the same.

RENFIELD'S REVENGE

I stopped and looked up at the red neon sign above the dark doorway – "Blood and Black Lace" – then back at my phone. Yep – my appointment was set for 9 p.m., and it was now 9:01. But the gallery looked closed, lights off and door locked.

I was about to try a phone call when I heard keys in a lock. I turned to see the door swinging open. "Del," said a woman's voice, deep and slightly husky, with an indefinable accent, "come on in."

I couldn't quite make out the voice's owner yet, but this had to Lilith Carville, who ran Blood and Black Lace with her husband Nathaniel. Although I'd been to their gallery when it had opened a month ago – they were only a mile from my store, Dark Delicacies – I'd never met the actual owners. Then, a week ago, I'd gotten the e-mail: they'd decided to move from dealing strictly in fine art to movie-making (hey, everybody in L.A. has to try the movie thing eventually, right?). They wanted to finance a movie called Renfield's Revenge. They knew I'd played Renfield more times than anyone else, but this time would be different because Renfield was the lead. I read their script and it wasn't bad, so we agreed to meet.

"I'm Lilith," she said, as she locked the door behind me and then turned to make her way through the dimly-lit gallery. I could just make out the framed pieces on the walls; their monstrosities and Gothic settings I remembered from my previous visit, but they somehow seemed even more menacing viewed in this light.

From what I could see of Lilith Carville, she was tall, built like an Aztec goddess, dressed in something tight and black. We reached a door at the rear of the gallery, went down a short hallway on the other side, and wound up in something that was probably supposed to be an office, but the word that came into my head was "lair". The walls were painted dark red, there was an antique secretary in one corner, its cubbyholes stuffed with papers, a glowing laptop on its desk, and most of the rest of the room was taken up with a black leather couch and two facing armchairs.

A man rose from the couch as we entered. "Del," he said, as he extended a hand. His voice had the same, slight accent that his wife's did, his hand was dry and so cool it was almost cold. Although this room was far from bright, it was well enough lit by an extravagant overhead chandelier that I could at least see them: the Carvilles were both striking looking, aside from their velvet-and-lace Goth-dandy outfits. They had gleaming brown skin, long, straight black hair, and a suggestion of confidence so strong it was almost arrogance. I hoped they wouldn't turn out to be just assholes.

After Nathaniel finished introducing himself, I was about to take the armchair he'd motioned to when I noticed the art in this room: it was different from what hung in the gallery, less hip and more Old Master-y. I walked up to examine the closest one, which showed a man bent over backwards, his throat exposed, while a woman with a crazed face and two-inch fangs knelt over him. Something about the style was familiar, it took me a few seconds... "Goya," I blurted out. "This looks like Goya, but I didn't know he ever painted a vampire scene."

"You've got a good eye, Del," purred Lilith.

"Nice print," I said.

Nathaniel agreed. "It is, isn't it?"

There were five more paintings hung around the room. They all showed vampire scenes, and they were all looked classical. *Hey, whatever*, I thought, *half my store's clientele has stuff like this in their homes.*

I sat, and they both looked at me intensely. After a few seconds, Lilith said, "So you liked the script?"

Considering that the script had her listed as writer, I chose my words carefully. "I've seen a lot of first drafts, but that one was really solid."

"Thank you," Lilith said, with a faint smile. "It was my first screenplay."

"Then that was a really good job. So this would be your first movie as producers, too?"

Nathaniel nodded. "That was one reason we wanted someone with your amount of experience."

Flattery usually works pretty well on me, but there were some alarm bells starting to go off. It took me a couple of seconds to figure out one thing that was bothering me: I'd been here for a couple of minutes now, and I was pretty sure that neither of them had blinked once.

Well, that and they hadn't offered me a beer.

"Do you have a director yet?" I asked.

They exchanged a look, then Nathaniel leaned forward; he didn't say anything, he just stared at me intently. *What the hell?* I was thinking. I started to wonder if they actually wanted to make porn and just didn't know how to ask.

After a while, Lilith set a small carton down on the coffee table between us; it was the kind of thing you'd get take-out noodles in, but whatever was in this wasn't noodles. I heard a skittering sound from inside the carton, and it jittered about on the table.

This was definitely getting weird. Nathaniel just kept staring at me, and Lilith was doing the same thing now. "*Pick up the carton, Del,*" she said.

Whatever was inside there, I was in no rush to see it. "I'll pass, thanks."

They both frowned; then Nathaniel said, his words commanding, "Pick up the carton, Del."

"Now why would I do that?"

"Because," Lilith said, "we want to see you eat what's in there."

Bug-eating. Renfield. Right.

"Sorry," I said, "but I'm not going Nicolas Cage for an audition."

Nathaniel blinked in dismay and leaned back. The two of them exchanged some angry words in another language; the argument ended when Lilith leaned forward, doing the staring thing now. A few seconds passed and she said, "Give us Dark Delicacies."

I was on my feet in a second. "I'm out of here –"

Instantly, Nathaniel was between me and the door, his lips pulled back to reveal nice long fangs. I looked at them for a moment before saying, "Good job on those – they almost look real. Now, get out of my way because I'm going."

Lilith joined her husband, looking perplexed. "You don't feel anything? Not even a little pull…?"

"You people are nuts." I pushed past them and rushed out into the hallway.

I'll admit I was a little unnerved; okay, I was *scared*. These people were whackjobs, and even if I made it to the front door I was still locked in.

Just as I reached the front they were there, laughing. "Del," said Nathaniel, "we're so sorry! We were just trying out some improv. We want to scare an *audience*, not you."

"Unlock the door, okay?"

Lilith did. As I walked out, I heard them shouting at each other in that language I didn't know.

When I got home, my wife Sue asked me how the meeting had gone. "I'm not sure," I said, "but I don't think they're even making a movie. I think they wanted our store. I'm pretty sure the whole thing was some kind of set-up to get Dark Delicacies."

The next day I called a guy who'd recently bought an authentic nineteenth-century vampire hunting kit from us and asked him if he knew anything about a couple named Nathaniel and Lilith Carville. He asked me to describe them, and gasped when I did. "Their last name isn't really Carville," he said. "It's something much older. You're lucky you got away. Did they try to hypnotize you?"

"Yeah, they did. It didn't work."

"I think it did once, but humans are more sophisticated these days. Thanks for the tip, Del – gotta run."

He hung up.

Later I drove by the Blood and Black Lace Gallery. I wasn't surprised to see a "For Lease" sign in the window.

Just when I was thinking they couldn't have been real vampires – the fangs had been good, but…real? – I thought about the paintings in their back room. I'd assumed they were prints, but now, looking back, I thought I remembered seeing actual swirls of paint. An original Goya no one else had ever seen?

I'd be a lot more careful in the future about who I auditioned for.

DRONE

Cheers, most important animal on earth, you think as you look at the bee and offer a toast. You try to remember where you heard that thing about bees being so high on the food chain, but you only know it was some post somewhere that you just skimmed past. Given how much tequila you've had in the last hour, it's a wonder you can remember that much.

You take another swig from your glass as you watch the insect flit among the tiny purple flowers on your rosemary bush.

Rosemary...about the only thing even you can't kill. Your nose burns as you snort derisively, a little of the tequila shooting up into your sinuses.

It's a beautiful spring day, which is why you're drinking alone outside in your backyard instead of inside. What else is there to do, after all, than sit outside soaking up alcohol and sun? You got laid off last year and hey, fuck all those reports about the hot economy because you haven't found a new job yet, and you've got just enough money to have a little more cheap booze delivered. You know you're lucky to have this house that Mom and Dad left you, but after a year of unemployed living you can't pay the property taxes.

You feel like a failure. You envy the bee, who still has a job and is good at it, gathering pollen on its little legs.

Maybe it's just the tequila, but the more you watch the bee, the more you notice odd things about it. It seems bigger than usual, for one thing – not as big as one of those huge furry bumblebees, but a half size up from the regular honey bee. Its main body is a brilliant gold, so bright that when the sun glints off of it, it hurts your eyes.

But it's not until the bee stops on a twig and seems to stare at you that you really start to wonder.

It just sits there, its legs twitching slightly, its reddish compound eyes seeming to gaze at you purposefully. You stare back, becoming uncomfortable. Shouldn't it be flying to the next flower already, gathering more pollen instead of just sitting there?

That's when you notice the blossoms it's already touched: they're withering, the violet petals turning brown as they curl in on themselves. They begin to fall as the nearby leaves wilt, the rosemary stems shrinking in on themselves.

You set your glass down, leaning forward. You don't know much about plants – gardening was Mom's thing, not yours – but you've never seen anything like this before.

That's when the bee leaves its perch, shoots forward, and stings you just below your right ear.

The pain is immediate and immense. You instinctively reach for your neck, where the skin is already fiery, with a lump rising. You haven't been stung by a bee since you were nine years old and one landed on your arm during summer camp; you don't remember it hurting this much. The site of the sting feels as if you've been stabbed with a red-hot blade, the pain is spreading throughout your head. You stagger to your feet, heading towards the house, wondering if you're having an allergic reaction, thinking maybe you should call 911 if you can only remember where you set down your phone –

The second sting comes then, this one just above your left eye. *I thought bees could only sting once*, rushes through your head before fresh agony drowns out thoughts.

It stings again, and again, on your arm, on your thigh below the shorts, on your bare ankle. It stings your side right through your t-shirt; it stings you between two fingers. You grasp at the frame of the back door and then you go down, unable to stand or move anymore. You fall onto your back, and there's the bee just above you, seeming magnified, its buzz deafening, waiting. It drops then, your eyes shutting an instant before it lands and you feel the sting in your left eyelid. Partly blinded now, you swing your hands wildly, but the bee avoids you easily.

And you're weakening. As the pain recedes, so does your ability to control your limbs. Within seconds you can barely lift your arms; no part of your body obeys you. Your consciousness drifts, freed now from sensation and demand. You're dimly aware of other things happening, other things changing. You feel lighter but more powerful, smaller but somehow greater.

The bees have changed, you think, and so will we.

You hear a voice now, but you realize you're not hearing it with *ears*, but something more primal. The voice doesn't speak words, but you understand it perfectly.

Purpose fills your being. You feel alive again, alive with meaning and belonging. As you lift yourself up, you've never felt so happy.

Welcome to the hive, says the wordless voice inside your new head.

THE WIND

Lupe looked up as another blast shook the two-bedroom house. The winds were getting stronger; when she'd checked the weather on her phone a few minutes ago, there'd been a warning of gusts up to 60 m.p.h. She knew her house was solid – "good bones," her papa had always said – but she had to wonder how long any structure could withstand these windstorms.

They'd gotten worse every year, along with the hot temperatures in the summer (115° was no longer unusual) and the dry winters. Up in the foothills, where Lupe's house was, it was even worse; she'd always imagined that the shallow ravine just above her must somehow channel and amplify the air currents.

Something was different tonight, though. It wasn't just the gusts that threatened to rip her trees out of the ground and scatter her chimney, that moaned and howled outside like living tortured things; no, there was something else in the air, something that made her shudder. Something...

Ouuuuuurrrrrssss...

Lupe turned the sound down on the television and then froze, listening. That sound, like a voice but not one she heard with her ears...

Another wail came, this one wordless, soundless, but enough to cause Lupe to flinch and pull her legs up into Papa's old easy chair.

Something was in the wind.

Forcing her legs to carry her, she rose and walked to the living room window, looking out into the night. It was dark except for the yellowish glow from the streetlights, leaves and papers whipping past her view, caught in the furious dance of air –

The air screamed.

Lupe instinctively pulled away from the glass, but forced herself to calm down.

You *know what this is,* she said to herself. *You've known all your life, like when you were four and you asked Tia Rosita who that man in the corner of her kitchen was, and she'd stared at you and muttered something under her breath as she crossed herself. Later on, many years later on, Mama told you that the man in the kitchen had been the ghost of Rosita's first husband, but by then you'd gotten used to seeing the ones that other people couldn't.*

She knew what it was that she heard in the wind.

Her house boomed as it was struck again. This time the power went out, leaving the room lit only by the distant glow of the streetlights. Lupe shivered in a howling darkness, her home surrounded by dead ones wafted on the wind.

She let sense-memory carry her along to the kitchen cabinet where she knew there were candles and matches. She found a short, vanilla-scented one in a shallow glass dish, lit it, and set it on the tiled counter as she sought to center herself. She willed her heart to slow, her consciousness to open to what was outside. She let the rage pour through and understood: *These are the ones who were here before us. Some, like mi familia, came here more recently; others were here long ago. Some are men, some women, some children; some were never human but animals; some were the spirits that were here long before the humans came. And they are all angry at what has been done to this place.*

Lupe wondered if the spirits were the wind, or the wind the spirits; had their anger created this storm, or had the storm awoken them? She didn't know, but sympathized with them, with what had been done to this place they had called home. It had changed so much in just the twenty-eight years since she'd been born here, even in just the five years since her Papa had died and she'd found herself living here alone.

Something huge crashed in the night, thudding against the front of the house. Lupe gasped as she realized what it had to be: her beloved acacia tree, the one she and Papa had planted when she'd been eleven, after the cancer had taken Mama. "This tree," Papa had said, "will be here for many years, long after I'm gone, even."

Lupe's own anger rose now. She went to the front door, unlocked it, and let the door blow open. The wind almost threw her back, but she fought against it as she thrust forward, to see the devastation for herself.

The acacia had been toppled; it now rolled, at an angle, along the edge of her roof, its majestic leafy bulk no more than a rag doll in this maelstrom. She felt tears torn from her eyes as she remembered its yellow blossoms, so thick and rich that standing beneath them as the bees crowded above was like being at the center of a benevolent heart.

Something in Lupe broke then. "NOOOOO," she shrieked against the wind, "I know you're angry, I know you think what's being done to your land isn't right, but neither is this. *You're hurting the land now.* STOP!"

She cried, not expecting an answer…but she got one nonetheless. The wind changed, no longer screaming along in a straight line but gathering in on itself, swirling around Lupe as she stood still.

A tornado. Or, as her Papa had called them, a dust devil. A spinning wall of air and spirits, with her at its eye.

It glowed slightly, sparks firing off, allowing Lupe to see the particles in the wind, and other, bigger things: the food wrappers and tissue paper and discarded mail that had cluttered the streets, branches and leaves, even battered lawn chairs and broken-legged tables.

Something dropped out of the vortex at her feet. Lupe looked down – and all the strength left her.

It was a child, a toddler, little more than a baby, dressed in tiny blue jeans and a torn t-shirt with a cartoon on the front. Lupe, whose legs had given way, stared at it for a few seconds, imagining someone's beloved little boy being torn from their grasp and whirled away. After a few seconds she looked up from where she knelt, crying out, "Now you kill children? How does this make you better? TELL ME HOW THIS HELPS."

The wind stopped.

There was a sound like a million leaves crunching underfoot as everything fell, and Lupe's inner sense, that one her Tia had been frightened of, told her that the spirits were gone.

She heard a small cry then, and felt her heart leap as she saw the toddler squirm. The boy was stunned, but got to his feet and began to sob. Lupe embraced him, letting her own tears mingle with his. She wondered if she'd just made a mistake when she'd assumed the child was dead, or if they'd felt shamed and called on their own magic to restore him. It didn't really matter either way.

The next time the winds came, she'd be ready for them.

THE PSYCHIC

Daria Parenti checked her make-up a last time in the lit mirror, looking up only when the dressing room door opened and her husband entered. "You about ready?" Carl asked.

She took a deep breath. "I guess. I just…it's one of those nights when I wish we were already in the hotel restaurant having a nice linguini and a glass of wine."

Carl put his hands on her shoulders. "I hear you, babe."

Daria smiled as she thought about how well he knew her. Carl might have been her manager for only two years, but he'd been her husband for fifteen. He knew when she wasn't feeling it.

Like tonight.

It actually wasn't *only* tonight. They hadn't talked about it yet, but Daria figured Carl knew by now that she hadn't been happy lately going out on stage, night after night, as "Daria Parenti, the People's Psychic." Every night, she stood under spotlights in a different city, staring out at hundreds of people who'd bought tickets because they were grieving or anxious or just curious, and then after giving what she could of herself, she and Carl went back to the latest hotel room – one exactly like another – and slept a few hours until they got in a car or on a plane and moved on to the next city. This had been their lives for six months now, and although the money was good – actually, it was *great*, way more than an Italian kid growing up in Jersey ever expected to see – Daria felt like she was being eroded, worn away.

The spirits were still there, just as they'd been there throughout Daria's life; she'd always heard them, clamoring for attention on the edge of awareness like dust flung against a window in a storm. As a child, her grandmother had told her about the "family gift", how it had skipped Daria's mother but landed strong in Daria, maybe stronger than it had been in anyone else. Grandmamma had the gift, too, and had taught Daria how to use it, to help others and protect herself. She hadn't thought about making a living from it, though, until she'd gained accidental fame three years ago by helping a friend find her missing child living in a trailer two hundred miles away with the ex-husband who'd taken her. Daria's talents had soon been greatly in demand, she'd written a book that had topped the Amazon bestseller charts for weeks, and Carl had finally suggested they both give up their jobs and turn this into a living.

It had worked…for a while. Not only was the money good, but Daria had ended each show feeling as if she'd given at least part of her audience some comfort. She saw how some of them cried during her readings, tears of mourning that turned to tears of joy.

And the spirits…they were more than ghostly presences to Daria. They were *companions*, there to ease her own discomforts. When Grandmamma had died last year, she'd been there every night, talking to Daria as if she stood right next to her, whispering in her ear.

But over the last few months, her spirit had dimmed. Or at least Daria had barely heard her. Daria knew it was her fault – she was tired, and bored, and drained, and not working as hard as she had in the beginning. She was skilled enough that she could skate through a performance offering her mourners intuition and solace, but she felt like she was letting them down. At least she was letting *herself* down.

"It's time," Carl said, waiting patiently.

Daria gave her make-up a last check, then rose and let Carl lead her to the stage. She barely heard the applause; she went into her performance by routine, calling the names and clues that entered her consciousness, letting a nervous widow or a depressed daughter know that Leo or Daddy still loved them from the other side.

You're nothing.

Daria stopped cold, startled by the words that had just sounded in her head. Still holding a microphone in one hand, she waited, silently, until it came again.

You're weak.

"I'm getting…" she broke off, not sure what she was getting.

Then: *you're going to die tonight.*

Daria was so startled she nearly dropped the mike; it made an amplified thump as she caught it. "Sorry, folks," she said, "but somebody who is very angry is trying to come through. Just a moment..."

She formed her thoughts, in the way Grandmamma had taught her, and sent out: Who are you?

A blast of pain rocked her.

Daria staggered, barely aware that the crowd gasped. She focused, searching, using her family gift to find and confront this spirit...

And then she was the one gasping, as she realized: this was not the spirit of someone who had passed on. It was someone here, in the audience, very much alive and determined to destroy her.

Why? she thought.

The response came back: Just to prove I can.

Another shot of agony rocked her. She cried out this time.

Carl started up onto the stage, but Daria held up a hand, and he stopped. No, she thought, *this is my fight.*

The voice came in answer: *You're old and used up. You can't fight me.*

Daria scanned the audience, the rows and rows of faces, all looking up at her anxiously, knowing something was wrong. They were mostly middle-aged and female, the ones who most needed someone, *anyone*, to tell them everything was fine, that they were loved, that they mattered. There were men, too, but not as many...

There. About six rows back, in an aisle seat – a teenage boy with greasy black hair and a t-shirt with an image of a bloody skull. As she spotted him, he gave her a mock salute.

He hit her with another blast. Daria felt real fear now; she wasn't sure how long she could withstand this boy, this powerful boy who could really destroy her.

Oh, I can and I will.

Daria knew then that she had one chance to defend herself. She mustered all of her gifts, calling out to the spirits, firming up her willpower and consciousness…

A voice sounded at her ear. *I'm here, granddaughter. Remember everything I taught you.*

Confidence and strength flowed through Daria. She felt the power grow within her, both an immovable object and an irresistible force. She closed her eyes for a few seconds, channeling everything within before she opened them again to stare at the teenage boy with greasy hair.

"That was some weird night, huh?" Carl said, just before taking another bite of his restaurant steak. "That audience got more than they bargained for."

You have no idea, Daria thought, but simply nodded.

"Whoever heard of an eighteen-year-old kid just keeling over dead from a brain aneurysm like that?"

Daria took another bite of her linguini, smiling. "That was weird," she agreed, "but I think things are about to get a lot better." She raised her glass, and Carl joined her. "To Grandmamma."

Her husband didn't completely understand, but he echoed her.

THE THINGS FINN LEFT BEHIND

Finn jolted awake as his phone's alarm went off. For a panicked few seconds, he had no idea where he was. Then he felt his cramped leg muscles, saw the windows surrounding him, and remembered: he was in the back seat of his car, which was tucked into a far corner of a shopping mall's parking structure. Since he'd managed to find a job as a bagger on the night shift at a supermarket, he'd needed someplace cool to park during the hot

Southern California days so he could sleep. His shift started in 30 minutes.

He sat up, ready to throw on his shoes and move up to the front seat, when something caused him to freeze; his nerves tingled in a way he hadn't felt since he'd left home a month ago.

Ten yards outside the car, near a dark stairway where the overhead light had gone out, was a dark, unmoving figure.

Finn peered at it, trying to quiet his racing pulse, trying to tell himself it was a security guard, or even just an optical illusion…but he felt this figure. It was more than an illusion.

He heard a voice outside the car then, something that sounded like a whisper he shouldn't have been able to hear…

Finnnnnn.

Closing his eyes tightly, Finn murmured, "No, no, no…"

When he opened his eyes again, the figure was gone, the space around the car silent.

Afraid now to step out of the car, he climbed over the seats and, fingers shaking, put the key in the ignition. The car radio blared to life, but the grungy rock song actually helped restore his calm, his sense that not everything was strange, abnormal.

He'd hoped he'd left all that behind when he'd fled Cedar Hill.

Finn had grown up – as pretty much every kid unlucky enough to be born in Cedar Hill had – hearing stories about strange things happening in his town. His grandma had used stories of a monster called Hoopsticks to scare him into being good. When he was six, his best friend Daphne told him that she'd seen strange creatures who had animal heads…and then she'd disappeared a week later. Finn still missed her.

But none of that had scared him as much as when Mom had brought Jim and Colin home six months ago and said they were all going to be living together.

Finn knew things had been hard on Mom ever since Dad had left for places unknown; Finn had been so young that he barely remembered his old man now. Mom had worked double-shifts at the drug store to keep a roof over their heads, and Finn had long ago gotten used to the kids at school taunting him over his secondhand clothes.

Then Jim had come into the drug store one day to pick up a prescription…and had left with Mom's phone number.

Finn actually didn't dislike Jim; his new stepfather (or, as Finn thought of him since he and Mom hadn't actually tied the knot, his *pseudo*-stepfather) for the most part ignored Finn, which was just fine.

No, it was Jim's son Colin who had immediately become Finn's personal supervillain. Colin was six months older than Finn but twice his size, and his favorite hobbies were casual cruelty, laughing at his own bad jokes, making threats, and sometimes indulging in actual physical harm. He'd broken Finn's right foot by "accidentally" dropping a brick on it one day when Finn had been working in the backyard. He'd decided to make his posse guffaw at school one day by punching Finn hard enough to give him a black eye. After a school counselor had reported the incident to Finn's mom, she'd taken him aside at home to tell him that he needed "to help make this family work."

And then there'd been Halloween.

Finn had turned 18 at the beginning of October and was already thinking of leaving; he stayed only because Grandma had urged him to finish high school. "Honey," she'd said last time he'd visited her in the nursing home, "you won't get anywhere in life without a high school diploma. Just tough it out until the end of the school year. I've got a little money tucked away and I can help then."

She'd given him her old car, since she couldn't drive any-more…and of course that had brought down the envious wrath of Colin.

Early on Halloween evening, Finn had breezed through the kitchen on his way to his friend Jeremy's house; Finn was going to drive them to a party, and he'd painted his face and splashed on some fake blood to go as a zombie. Colin stood in front of the kitchen sink, using a knife to cut apple slices. "What are you supposed to be – road kill?"

Finn had been intending to get some water, but instead turned; he could get a drink at Jeremy's house.

He was walking away when a hand on his arm yanked him roughly back. "Hey, I asked you a question."

Finn answered, "I'm a zombie."

"A zombie, huh?" Colin pretended to eye Finn's make-up, but then the knife shot up and drew a jagged line across Finn's cheek. "There, that's better."

Finn blinked in pain as his hand shot to his face, fingers coming away covered in *real* blood. Finn looked up just in time to see Colin stepping forward, saying, "But let's make sure you win the Best Costume award –"

He swung the knife at Finn's midsection. Finn reacted in-stinctively, staggering back –

Something happened. Finn still didn't remember clearly, but the next thing he knew, Colin was on the kitchen floor with the knife sticking out of his belly, gasping like a gutted fish. He died in the ambulance fifteen minutes later.

His death was ruled accidental – he'd apparently slipped on a dropped apple slice – but Jim had ordered Finn out of the house as Mom stood by silently. He'd been only to happy to pack a few things in the car, pay one last visit to Grandma (who wrote him a check), and drive. He just wanted to put Cedar Hill as far behind him as possible, go someplace that was warm and safe and not full of monsters.

He drove west until the Pacific Ocean stopped him. Once there, he didn't mind living in his car until he could save up some more money. He got a job bagging groceries at a store in Redondo Beach, and he liked the hard work. He would save up enough to maybe share an apartment, then get his GED, maybe even go to college someday. Everything was okay for a few weeks…

But the day after he saw the dark figure in the parking structure, he woke up to find the windows of the car covered in handprints that faded as he watched.

The next day he was jolted out of sleep when the car rocked up and down. He didn't have to look to know there was no one outside.

Two nights later, as he sat in the front getting ready for work, he saw a face in the rearview mirror.

It was Colin.

He'd already guessed his tormentor's identity, of course. He blurted out the name, but there was no response.

Finn knew then that he hadn't really escaped Cedar Hill; the town had followed him here, as unshakeable as a bad hangover. Colin was clearly not finished with him.

Two nights later, Finn awoke in the back seat with that sense that he was being watched. It seemed darker than usual, the shadows thicker…especially in the car's front seat, where a dark mass sat behind the wheel, turned in his direction.

In that instant, Finn understood that this thing would follow him forever unless he stood up to it. He sat up, quivering with energy that he finally let loose.

"You know what, Colin? You were a pathetic loser in life, and you're twice as pathetic in death. You're a bully who caused his own death, and now you just want to hit someone 'cause you're so pissed off, but you can't even do that. Do you think any of this shit scares me? It doesn't, you don't, you never will, and you need to move on NOW, so get the fuck out of my car and don't come back."

The effect was instantaneous: the figure vanished, the car filled with light, and the change in the very air was palpable. Finn knew he'd won.

He hoped Colin had gone back to Cedar Hill. Finn, on the other hand, had now left that haunted place behind forever.

ONE SHOT

After I got my vaccination, I felt safer.

Of course that didn't change the fact that I'd lost Jack.

We'd only been married for six months when the virus hit. I remember those first few anxious months barricaded away in our apartment, trying to be happy in a world that was anything but. We became news junkies. We explored delivery options. We ate our entire supply of canned goods and got by on whatever we could get after. Jack was usually the one who did our shopping runs; I was always nervous until he got home again. He'd be depressed because he'd only been able to get a few things we needed; the markets were running out of essentials. But we comforted each other, and we hung in there together.

At least it was never like it was in the movies; there was no mass collapse of society. There were even good things to come out of it: communities bonded together to protect themselves. We finally got to know all of our neighbors in the apartment complex; we learned which ones were dependable and would actually stick to their assigned shifts, and which ones were likeliest to endanger us all. I learned how to shoot, and the government kept us supplied with bullets. When I killed my first zombie, it was a strange experience: on the one hand, I was surprised with my own shooting skills and was proud for protecting myself and my group, but I couldn't shake the feeling that I'd just murdered someone's sister or wife or mother.

Things slowly eased up, though. Barricades built around cities worked, and smaller communities no longer had to adhere to such rigid protections. Enough people had died in the first wave that housing prices plummeted, and even though Jack was unemployed my job as an IT specialist allowed us to buy a house, complete with its own nice backyard office. We couldn't possibly have afforded the place a year ago.

One day the government announced a vaccine. It wouldn't cure anyone who'd already been bitten by a zombie and turned, but it would protect the living; a bite would now be a treatable injury, not a death (and beyond) sentence.

We waited our turn. And waited.

One day Jack came to me and said it was time for him to contribute, that he could no longer in good conscience let me be the sole breadwinner. I agreed…until he told me he'd just taken a job with the newly formed City Patrol Corps. The CPC manned the barricades, took out approaching zombies, and disposed of the remains. I begged him not to take the job until he got vaccinated, but he told me that signing up with CPC would mean we'd *both* get jumped to the front of the vaccination line. His friend Armando was with the CPC, and said the work was easy and the pay was great.

He signed up. They gave him a day of training, told him the vaccine supply was still short but we'd get our shots next week. They threw him into the front lines.

He came home on his third day and rolled back his sleeve to show me the wound.

It wasn't deep, was barely bleeding…but he'd been surprised by a zombie that had come from within the city, quietly, marching up behind him when his partner was on a break. It had grabbed his arm and bitten him before he could do anything. He'd shot it, and then covered up the bite. Because, of course, if he'd admitted that, he would've been taken to a "quiet room" and shot in the head.

He'd come home, instead. He was already starting to feel feverish. He called and quit the job while he was still lucid.

I knew from all that news-watching we'd done that we had two days at the most until he turned. I also knew it was illegal not to report the bite.

I didn't care. I wasn't going to lose Jack, not this soon.

I tucked him into bed, ran to the bank, took out a substantial amount of cash, and then went to the hardware store. Twelve hours later, the backyard office was soundproofed and safe. My plan was simple: I'd keep Jack back there until they developed a way of curing zombification. I had no idea how I'd feed him, but I'd figure something out.

He died the following day. I dragged his body to the office, put a chain around his ankle for double safety, checked the boards over the windows and the lock on the door, and then I waited.

He turned an hour later. He was hungry when he awoke, looking pale and gaunt, and he lunged for me. The chain pulled him back and he started to wail. Alarmed, I slammed the door shut before any of the neighbors could hear. If I got caught, I was looking at a felony charge.

I kept him that way for a few weeks. I tried feeding him raw beef, but he slapped it aside and angrily grabbed at me again… and again…and again. I began to wonder if I'd made a terrible mistake. In the meantime, I finally got my vaccination, so if I slipped up and he got to me, at least I'd survive.

Then my internet research began to lead me down a new rabbit hole: there was a lot of speculation about what would happen if a zombie received the vaccination. The government had made that completely illegal – it was just as big a crime as keeping a zombie – but they didn't say why. There were a lot of theories out there, but the most popular one was that it would return humanity to a zombie, but leave them with all of the rot and bodily damage they'd suffered. That might explain the criminal charge – even if the victim survived all that agony, their resulting healthcare would drain resources fast.

I thought about that a lot. Jack hadn't been dead all that long; it was cold in the backyard office, so he hadn't suffered much rot yet. And his initial wound had been inconsequential.

I was willing to try it.

I had a friend who was a nurse; I told her my 85-year-old neighbor was bedridden but I could give her a vaccination. Hospitals and clinics were overwhelmed, so my friend didn't ask too many questions, just made sure I knew how to use a syringe.

I thought about the best way to do it. I'd have to distract him and be quick with the shot. Even though I'd been vaccinated, he could still kill me if I wasn't careful.

I came up with a plan. It was simple: I'd unlock the office door, let him come for me, then throw a steak into the corner. I knew he'd investigate. While his back was to me, I'd jab him, then step back and wait.

The plan actually worked. I got him the shot. I stood outside the door, waiting.

It didn't take long. The hunger faded from him. The expression of ravenous fury fell away. He dropped to the floor, the chain rattling. After a few minutes he looked up at me and called my name.

I began to cry. It was Jack, my Jack. I'd saved him.

He seemed weak, but I'd expected that. He said the chain was weighing him down. He wanted to get up and come back into the house. "Of course," I said, fishing the key to his handcuff out of a pocket. I had to wipe away tears as I unlocked him. He smelled bad, but I knew we could clean him up when he was inside.

As soon as the chain fell to the floor, he attacked. "I'm so sorry," he said, as he tore a chunk out of my shoulder, "but I have to do this."

I ran, made it to the house, locked all the doors. He's out there now, pounding on the sliding glass patio door, telling me he's sorry, that he loves me.

If anyone reads this, just know that there's a reason you shouldn't give the vaccine to a zombie: because it doesn't cure the hunger, but it brings back their minds. What I've just done should be a felony.

I just hope they let Jack live.

POPPIES

Jazmyn stood next to her mini-Coop, staring out at the endless sea of orange blossoms.

"Okay," Shaun said from the other side of the car, "I gotta say that's beautiful."

She nodded, and he knew she was probably glad he'd said that. He hadn't really wanted to come on this drive – 90 minutes from Silverlake, up into the foothills where the California poppies were in full bloom – but she'd promised him lunch afterwards at his favorite taco joint and he'd acquiesced. Besides, not as if he had much else to do, since he'd been an unemployed barista for the last two months.

The field of golden flowers was separated from the winding two-lane highway by a low picket fence; signs were spaced along that border reading "NO TRESPASSING" and "PLEASE DO NOT CROSS FENCE."

Jazmyn raised a leg in preparation for stepping over the pickets.

"What are you doing?" asked Shaun, mildly alarmed but also amused.

"C'mon, we drove all the way up here, so let's run through the field, like Julie Andrews in *The Sound of Music*."

"I think she was running across grass in the Alps, Jaz."

"Whatever." Jazmyn stepped over the fence and stood in the field. The poppies came almost up to her knees, the growth so dense that her feet were lost from view. "Dude, let's do this."

Something itched at Shaun like a tick digging in. He looked around, his uneasiness growing. "Where is everyone else? Isn't this whole poppy thing huge in the news?"

Jazmyn shrugged. "That's why I picked a Monday morning. Yesterday it was probably jammed."

Shaun finally figured out what was bothering him: it was the cars. They lined both sides of the highway, pulled over on the dirt shoulders next to the picket fences; a lot of them were SUVs, meaning families were here…or *had* been. "If nobody's here today, what's with all the cars?"

Jazmyn was getting irritated. "I don't know – maybe people park here to car-pool or something. Who cares? Come on!" She turned and started running through the poppies, their orange heads nodding and parting before her.

Shaun reluctantly stepped over the fence. The ground on the other side was surprisingly soft underfoot, not hard-packed like the clay soil of the shoulder. He took a few steps forward, finally breaking into a jog to reach his friend.

"I love this!" Jazmyn called, running across the field with her arms widespread.

Shaun ran forward a few feet then stopped, taking in the surroundings. He turned 360 degrees, seeing poppies in every direction. He remembered being frightened by the poppy scene from *The Wizard of Oz* as a child, but those poppies hadn't been orange like these. He inhaled deeply, surprised by the slight scent of something musky, almost…*meaty*.

He saw that Jazmyn had stopped running and was looking down. "What?" Shaun called to her.

She bent down, scrutinizing the greenery beneath the orange. "I just tripped on something…"

Shaun took one step towards her – and gasped as his right foot sank into the earth. He yanked it back, but it was caught on something. He pulled harder and it came free. He raised it to look, balancing on one leg, and saw some sort of brownish, dirt-covered root still wrapped around the toes of his sneakers. "Huh?" he said to himself, wondering how the root could have wrapped all the way around his foot in a split second.

Shivering in the warm, still air, Shaun shouted to Jazmyn, "What if there are snakes or scorpions or something out here?"

To his surprise Jazmyn didn't laugh the suggestion off. "Maybe…" she said, looking around her own feet.

"I'm going back," Shaun said, before he tripped and went down.

His hands landed on something moist and squishy buried below the poppies, something that didn't feel like soil. He grabbed a mass in his right hand and pulled it free to examine.

It was a dirt clod, the size of a softball, something pale just visible beneath the dark brown. Shaun shook it to remove some of the dirt, crying out as he saw what was plainly part of a human hand with two fingers still attached. He dropped the gruesome remains in shock, leapt to his feet, and turned to see Jazmyn making her way towards him. "Fuck, Jaz, I just found part of a hand."

"Part of a what –?" She broke off as her legs were pulled out from under her and she went down, half-hidden beneath the poppies.

"Jaz!" Shaun shouted her name over and over and started to run towards her. Jazmyn began to scream, her hands flailing.

Shaun was twenty feet from reaching her when his own ankles were grabbed and he fell. He began tearing at his feet, finding them entwined by thick, ropy roots that were pulling him down into the spongy ground. His hands grabbed frantically, and felt more of that stuff beneath him that was neither dirt nor plant, and he knew then what had happened to the people who had been in all those cars. *Fertilizer*, he thought as he struggled.

Shaun fought, thrashing and fighting his way to a standing position. He realized Jazmyn had stopped screaming, and one glance back showed no sign of her, only a slight depression in the poppies where he thought she'd been.

He turned back in the direction of the road, maybe fifty feet away. He already felt his legs being circled again, he began kicking and pulling at roots, which wrapped around his hands, he knew he didn't have long left unless –

He saw a police car cruise along the two-lane highway and stop. He shrieked for help, trying desperately to raise his arms.

Two uniformed cops got out of the car.

"Help me!" Shaun screamed, "HELP — !"

The cops stood beside their cruiser, watching impassively.

Shaun tried to scream again, but there was a root in his mouth, gagging him.

The last thing he saw was the cops, standing safely on the asphalt, directing the arriving tow trucks to remove the cars.

THE FACE IN THE FRAME

I made a mistake. A *terrible* mistake. I see that now.

At the time, it was just…research. I'd found a trail, was on the hunt for a story. But I got too close. And now…

First, you should know how it started.

My name is Elspeth Giraudoux. My friend's call me Elle. I've got a BA in Journalism and a Masters in Film; I got those little pieces of paper a while back, so I've been teaching and writing about film for some years now. My specialty is old horror movies. When I say, old, I mean OLD – silents and early talkies. I can tell you whatever you want to know about Lon Chaney (Senior, not the Wolf Kid), Conrad Veidt, Edison's *Frankenstein*, or the original *Phantom of the Opera*. Everybody knows about those; my reputation has been built on tracking down the weird ones, the lesser known gems. A lot of them are lost now, but enough are still around to make it interesting.

It started with a 1917 two-reeler called *The Hostess and the Ghostess*. It was a silly comedy starring Mabel Normand as a woman who inherits a haunted house; at first we think the ghost is a conniving lawyer who knows there's oil under the house and he wants to scare her so badly he can buy it cheap, but then it turns out there's a real ghost in the house, and it likes Mabel more than the lawyer. Sounds innocent enough, right?

I was preparing a paper (the title was long and pretentious and you don't need to know it) on how ghosts had changed in movies since the silents, and this one was a classic example of the "cut two eye-holes in a white sheet" style of ghost costume, so I decided to use it in the paper. There was a scene that was surprisingly still unnerving, when the ghost fades in at the end of a long, dark hallway. I actually wasn't sure how they'd done it – was it just a superimposition, or was it something like the Pepper's Ghost illusion with a carefully-positioned sheet of glass? I was leaning toward my television screen, streaming the movie from the Library of Congress website, when I first saw it.

It was a face, peering out from one of the side doors in the hallway. It was a small face, but utterly horrifying, with bulging eyes, a grin that reached all the way to the pointed ears, a gaping cavity where the nose should've been, and a gleaming, hairless pate that looked like a skull. It just suddenly appeared in one frame – no fade in – lasted exactly three frames, and then vanished again.

I'd never seen anything like that face; the closest I could come was Max Schreck's vampire in *Nosferatu*, but this face was even worse. It seemed inhuman, completely mad, like some kind of crazed animal. It didn't look like a mask, but I couldn't imagine what else it might be, or why it was there. Was it some sort of early experiment with subliminal images, like the face of the demon in *The Exorcist*?

I brought up the movie on my computer, printed out an image of the face, and sent it to a few colleagues, but everyone else was as baffled as I was. I taped the print-out to the wall above my desk, even though just touching the picture made me shiver.

I chalked it up to some anomaly I could always come back to and moved on. A few weeks later I was watching episode 4 of a 1939 serial called *Ghost Wranglers* (about a cowboy hero helping a woman who thinks the ranch she's just inherited is haunted) that I'd found on YouTube, when I saw the face again. This time it popped up in an otherwise-innocent scene, as the hero was saddling up in the barn. It was in the back of the shot, just visible in the shadows under a hay loft.

I nearly jumped a mile when it flashed by, then grabbed my remote, rewound the movie a few seconds, and watched again.

It was absolutely the same face. As with the silent film, it was in there maybe four, five frames total, meaning most people would never have noticed it, but I'm always looking for details I can write about in these films.

These movies were made 22 years apart; why would it have appeared in both of them? One flick with that thing was weird enough, but two…well, there had to be a common factor.

I got together every fact I could about *The Hostess and the Ghostess* and *Ghost Wranglers*, and found exactly one thing they had in common: they'd both been made at a lot in Hollywood called JoMar Studios. I looked up JoMar, found out they'd started in 1916 – one year before *The Hostess and the Ghostess* – and had finally been demolished in 1962. Where they'd once been was now an office building.

Researching JoMar wasn't easy. I found it that it was started by two investors, Joe Levant and Marcus Ailsbert, who cleverly combined their first names to create their studio moniker. Their lot had housed two soundstages, and if Joe and Marc had ever had ambitions about making it big in Hollywood, they must've given up early on and just rented JoMar to B-pictures. By the 1950s it had gained a reputation for being rundown, dirt cheap...and haunted.

Yes, haunted. I found a blog that went into the history of it, had the usual crap about how it had been built in an area that the native Tongva people had thought was the home of an evil forest spirit, nobody liked to work at JoMar because it had a "bad atmosphere," and a lot of people were glad when it was finally torn down.

The last production shot at JoMar in '62 was an exploitation "gang of juvenile delinquents" thing called Eighteen and Evil that was available on DVD from a company that specialized in grindhouse cinema. The DVD arrived, I put it in, got close to the television set...

And there it was: the face appeared eighteen minutes in, looking out from behind a couch as two kids made out in front of it, apparently oblivious. This time it was there for seven frames.

I knew then that I'd find it in every movie made at JoMar.

What was strange was that I couldn't find any reported sightings of anything like that being spotted in person. Sure, there were lots of paranormal reports from JoMar's history...but if anybody had come across this thing outside their dressing room or on a stage late at night, it would've been Hollywood folklore.

I've always liked the idea of believing in ghosts even if I wasn't 100% convinced…but this was no ghost. This didn't even look human. I was going with the evil forest spirit thing, although I also found that paranormal experts sometimes called *Big Bads* like this "elementals".

I decided it was an elemental that could only be seen on film.

So what had happened to it after JoMar had been demolished? I couldn't find any instances of paranormal happenings reported from the office building that now occupied that location; in fact, it might've been the only structure in Hollywood that didn't seem to be haunted.

It was almost as if it had been captured in the film, trapped there, until…

Someone saw it.

Me.

In case you're thinking, "Hey, Elle, you've got a heckuva paper to write now," let me assure you that I will never write that paper.

Why? you may be asking.

I'll tell you why: because tonight I turned on my television, planning to relax by binging some mindless Netflix series…

And the first image that came up on the screen was it.

It's still there now, staring at me, even after I turned the television off and disconnected the power. It was trapped in the JoMar movies, but somehow my recognizing it must have freed it.

I'm writing this blog and posting it so someone will know what happened to me, in case.

In case it gets loose, and comes after me.

And then comes after…whoever's next.

THE PODCAST

"So," Megan said to her guest of the week, "your bio says that you're dead."

"That's right," said the man on the other half of Megan's screen. His name was Byron Croft, and he was completely unremarkable looking: early thirties, short dark hair, a few light scars that were testament to an acne-laden youth. He'd recently hit occult bestseller lists with a book called *Spell Them: An Authentic*

Grimoire, so producer Jax had booked him for Megan's paranormal podcast, *Into the Dark with Megan Barnham.*

Laughing (because Megan knew her fans liked it when she laughed), Megan said, "But you don't look dead."

"Well, I am. Do I look 78 years old?"

"No. You look maybe 32."

Croft smiled. "Good guess, because that's how old I was when I died."

"So that was," Megan did a quick calculation in her head, "46 years ago?"

"Yep."

"So was this during surgery, or…?"

"Oh, no no no." Croft leaned forward slightly, and Megan noticed that he seemed to either be in some place very dark, or the wall behind him was painted black. "No, I sacrificed myself to the Dark Lord."

Megan almost groaned, thinking, *Oh, great, this guy's a whackjob. Why isn't Jax vetting these guys before inviting them onto the show?* Instead, she said, "Wow. That sounds painful."

"It was – I had to use a consecrated blade that I really should've sharpened more – but it was worth it, because I'll live forever and never feel pain again."

"Is this all detailed in your book?"

Croft's smile widened to a grin, an expression that probably looked creepier than it really was on Megan's computer screen. "No, I didn't put *everything* into the book. I mean, it wouldn't do to have everyone living forever, right?"

"Uhhh…right." Megan glanced at her notes, wondering how she was going to fill an entire hour with this guy's ranting. "So tell us about some of the spells that you did include in the book."

"Oh, you know, the usual: love spells, how to get money, how to take out an enemy, how to change your appearance, things like that."

"'How to change your appearance'? Oh, I could use that!" Megan laughed again.

Croft didn't. "Would you like to see a demonstration?"

Megan abruptly felt a chill, but she didn't let on. "Sure."

"I thought you might. So I got a few items together…" Croft reached out of frame, held up a small metal bowl, a glass bottle with stopper, and a knife. "I've got some herbs here, a few oils in the bottle, and my athame."

"Tell everyone what an 'athame' is, Byron."

"It's a ceremonial dagger."

"Is that the same one you used to sacrifice yourself?"

"As a matter of fact, it is. This time I made sure it was nice and sharp, though." Croft set the dagger down, pulled the stopper from the bottle, and poured the light green contents into the bowl. "First we add the oils to the herbs…"

"What herbs exactly?"

"Oh, you'll have to buy the book to find that out."

Megan wanted to groan again, but said, "Gotcha."

Next, Croft used the athame to slice open his left palm. "Now a little blood, because a sacrifice is always required, and lastly the incantation…" He closed his eyes and began to mutter something under his breath. Megan couldn't make it out, but thought it was Latin. Croft finished in a few more seconds, and opened his eyes to smile into his camera. "That's it."

Megan peered at the screen, but nothing was happening. She'd at least expected a cheap special effect or magic trick. "So what –"

She broke off as Croft began to change. His features became bigger and coarser, his hair and eyebrow grew out, his skin reddened, his ears lengthened to points. Megan had to admit it was impressive, more than what she'd expected. "Oh," she blurted out, "wow. What are you supposed to be, Byron?"

When he spoke again, his voice sounded deeper, more like an animal growl. "This is my true appearance. Or has been, ever since I gave my soul to His Infernal Majesty."

Megan brought up the "chat" function on her computer, and typed a private message to her producer: *Jax, what's with this guy?*

The response came back instantly: Sorry, *he wasn't like this in the pre-interview. Just try to ride it out.*

Turning her attention back to the screen, Megan said, "Okay, so that's pretty good. What are some of the other spells?"

He laughed, and the sound was guttural, repulsive. He reached down out of screen, and held up a larger bowl, this one inscribed with arcane symbols and handles carved like demon heads. He began reciting loud and fast in a language Megan couldn't identify; he gestured at the bowl, and whatever it held burst into flames…that screamed.

"Okay, this is too weird," Megan cried out. "Jax, I'm sorry, but I'm shutting this down."

Her producer's image popped onto her screen. "I'm with ya, Megs. I'm…uhhh…" He frowned, looking down, concerned.

"What?" she asked.

"This is weird…I can't seem to shut this thing down…"

On the screen, Byron Croft finished his recitation and threw his head back to howl laughter. Megan used her mouse to stab randomly at buttons on the screen, but nothing ended the call. "Jax, what's going on?"

Croft stopped laughing long enough to lean closer to the screen, and Megan involuntarily drew away from hers. "I'll tell you what's going on: I've just summoned demons and released them on every single person who hears this."

"Oh yeah?" Megan found a reserve of courage and addressed Croft angrily. "You forgot something, asshole: the podcast is pre-recorded. Nothing's going to happen if we don't upload it."

Croft just roared before abruptly vanishing, leaving only Megan and Jax on the screen – and Jax went pale. "What?" Megan asked.

"I don't understand how this is happening, but…*the podcast just uploaded itself.*"

Megan heard a sound coming from her office behind her, a sound like nails – or claws – on wood.

Her scream was the last thing the podcast recorded.

THE LEGION

"Good Lord, Sarah – an entire legion of ghosts? Don't you think that seems a bit unlikely in 1880?" Hugh smiled and stroked the upturned, waxed end of his moustache to show his friend that he was being playful.

Sarah arched an eyebrow and sipped from her tea. "I didn't say that I saw any such thing. I'm merely reporting what was said to me by someone else."

"Said to you by someone else at the séance you attended last night, you mean."

Squirming slightly, Sarah answered, "Yes, I was at a séance, and yes, I believe in the possibility of spirits." She waved a gloved hand around the elegant tea-room, indicating the well-dressed customers. "As, no doubt, do many of those around us."

Hugh followed her glance and then smirked. "Britain's elite do seem to be smitten by the insubstantial of late."

"You don't believe any of it, Hugh?"

His moustache twitching, Hugh answered, "Sorry, old girl, I don't. We live in an age when we could capture incontrovertible proof of such things if they existed, but no such proof has been offered yet."

"But think of the possibility: what if they do exist, outside the boundaries of normal space and time? Remember how in olden times they used to call on ghosts for prophecies? It was because ghosts are timeless. That's why they can't be captured by our primitive methods."

Shaking his head, Hugh answered, "I'm still not about to believe in two-thousand-year-old Roman soldiers traipsing about the moors."

"Don't you see, though? They don't know that two thousand years have passed, because they're outside of time." When Hugh didn't answer, Sarah tried a different approach. "What if you personally witnessed something? Would that change your mind?"

Hugh peered at her for an instant before asking, "Are you suggesting something?"

"Lord Adair told me last night that he'd seen the ghostly legion parading along the old Roman road that cuts across the moors near Scarborough. Let's go there, Hugh."

He considered carefully before answering. Sarah had been his closest friend since childhood; even then she'd believed in fairies and witches and ghosts while Hugh never had. But he had a holiday coming up, with no plans, and he did enjoy their trips together. "All right," he said, his agreement causing Sarah's face to light up with glee. "Let's go meet your Roman ghosts."

A week later, they'd hired a carriage to take them from their hotel in Scarborough out to the moors. It was after ten at night, and although the moon had been high when they'd left town, the moors were shrouded in thick fog and a chill that made them pull their coats tighter. The driver agreed to wait; Hugh noticed him tilting a flask up as he huddled on the carriage's front bench. The horses' breath sent up clouds of steam as they pawed the ground restlessly.

Hugh held up a lantern as they ambled a short way down the ancient road, little more than a muddy track dividing the moors. Looking behind them, he realized that the fog was so dense they'd lost sight of the carriage after just a hundred feet. "We need to be cautious, my dear," Hugh said to Sarah, "wouldn't do to get turned around out here."

"We only need to follow the road back," she said.

Hugh paused in the middle of road, moving the lantern around. "How far do you think we need to go?"

Sarah peered about, unable to see beyond a few yards. "I suppose here's as good as anywhere. The legends say the legion appears around eleven at night."

Hugh pulled out his watch. "We've got twenty minutes, then." Tucking the watch back in his pocket, he reflexively stroked his moustache, which had begun to droop in the moist air.

As Sarah paced the road in anticipation, Hugh found himself regarding her with affection…and some regret. They'd known each other since they could remember, their houses next to each other in Lewes. They'd stayed close throughout the years, written each other weekly letters when they were apart at school, gotten together for lunches and dinners now that he was a solicitor in London and she tutored children of the wealthy…and Hugh supposed that both their families expected them to marry.

He only hoped that Sarah didn't expect that as well, because…it would never happen. It wasn't that Hugh didn't love her, but he loved her as a friend, nothing more. He couldn't fancy ever fancying her, not in that way. Put very simply, Hugh wasn't interested in women at all, and he knew that someday he must tell Sarah…unless she'd already guessed his secret. If she had, she'd been blessedly discreet because it was a secret that could destroy his career and life.

"What time is it now?" she asked.

Hugh checked his watch again. "Two minutes until eleven."

A silence fell over them, until Sarah turned to look up at Hugh. "Hugh, there's something I've been wanting to tell you…"

Oh no, he thought. *I shall have to reveal my secret tonight.* This wasn't how he'd planned to do this – on a dank, lonely moor late at night.

He gulped and said, "Yes?"

"I…"

Hugh heard something, then, a distant rumble. He frowned, trying to place the sound. Sarah saw his expression and asked, "Hugh? What…?"

"Do you hear that?"

She listened, and then looked back at him. "No, I don't…"

"It's like some sort of…great engine…"

Something was coming towards them: two bright lights, cutting through the fog along with that sound. Hugh instinctively stepped back off the road just as something rushed, something like a small train car but on its own four wheels, without a track, the lights mounted to the front of it. Hugh cried out in shock as it swept by, vanishing in the fog, that terrible sound fading.

Sarah stood nearby, staring not at the road but at him, her eyes wide. "Hugh…?"

"Didn't you see that?" He glanced at her, saw from her expression that she didn't.

Then Sarah faded away.

The fog and the moors vanished as well, replaced by an urban street, but unlike any street Hugh had ever seen. The buildings were glass and metal, of designs he didn't recognize. There were more of the metal carriages racing along, and the air stank of fuel. It was night, but electric streetlights lit the scene well, far better than the gaslights of London. As Hugh watched, stunned, two men strolled by, dressed in sleek clothes that exposed their arms and heads…and even more startling, the men stopped before him and embraced.

One of them looked up at Hugh and his jaw dropped. He pulled away from the other man and stared, mute, until his companion saw the expression. "What is it, darling?"

"There…" He pointed at Hugh, who stood frozen.

The other man looked, squinted, but said, "I don't see anything."

"It was a man, with a long moustache, and wearing old clothes…bloody hell, Martin, I think I just saw a ghost."

And then, in the blink of an eye, the men, the street, the buildings, the carriages, the electric lights were gone, replaced by the fog and the moor and Sarah, staring wide-eyed at Hugh, who panted for breath.

"Are you all right, Hugh?" she asked.

He laughed nervously before replying, "What did I just see?"

He knew, then: Sarah had been right, that ghosts were outside of regular space and time, and he'd just had a glimpse of the future, where nights were brightened by electricity, and men like him no longer held terrible secrets.

He turned to Sarah. "It's after eleven. Let's go back."

Sarah nodded sadly, disappointed at glimpsing no transparent legion, and began trudging towards their carriage.

"Oh," Hugh called after her, "was there something you were going to tell me?"

She stopped, turned, he saw her anxiety as she said, "Yes… I've…well, Hugh, I've met someone, someone very special…"

Hugh didn't hear the rest; he was overwhelmed by relief, and joy for her, and hope for the future. When she stopped, he took her hand and said, "My dear, I'm so very happy for you."

"Are you crying?"

"Yes, I believe I am. Now let's get back to our hotel, it's bloody freezing out here."

She let him lead the way back.

JUST ONE MORE

"Hi, my name is Dave, and…well, I'm not an alcoholic yet…"

Aram, who ran the liquor store at the end of Dave's block, looked up and smiled, but the expression was tired. Dave thought everything Aram did must be tired; the man seemed to work 168 hours a week in the store.

"How are you tonight, my friend?" Aram asked in his soft, slightly accented voice.

Dave shrugged. "Hey, for a guy who's been out of work for five months now and whose girlfriend isn't very happy, I'm just great." He walked to the beer section, peering through the cool glass. He usually grabbed two six-packs of whatever was on sale, but he stopped when something new caught his eye: a craft beer called Scratch Ale, with a label that had catchy, bright artwork of a crimson-skinned imp looking amusingly toasted. Curious, Dave opened the door and pulled out a bottle, eyeing the label.

"New local brewery," Aram said behind him.

Dave grunted, raising the beer to read the brewery's name: Lew's C4 Brewery. "What's a 'C4 Brewery'?" he muttered.

Aram heard and answered, "I don't know, but I've been selling those like crazy."

"What the hell," Dave said, "I'll give it a shot. I like to support the local guys." He bought two six-packs, told Aram not to work too hard, and walked the block back to his apartment.

His girlfriend Brittney was on the couch, laptop open before her as she Zoomed with friends. She glanced up as he walked in, put the laptop on mute, and looked pointedly at the six-pack in each hand. "Really, Dave?" She'd been on him for a while about how much he was drinking.

He raised one of the cartons. "Aram says it's a new local brewery. Might as well give the locals a little love, right?"

"Sure. Hey, maybe *they'll* give you a job."

Dave didn't answer; instead he headed for their six-by-six-foot patio, leaving Brittney to tell her girlfriends about how worried she was.

Sighing, Dave fell into the lawn chair surrounded by some dying potted palms, reached down, pulled out the first bottle, twisted the cap off, took his first gulp –

The world melted away. Within seconds, Dave felt things he'd never even imagined: his cotton t-shirt caressed his chest like the finest silk, the glass against his lips felt like the tongue of a goddess, the night air was no longer congested with the pollution of a nearby freeway but was instead scented like an unimaginably expensive perfume. He nearly dropped the bottle in surprise, but tightened his grip and raised it again. The cool liquid moved through him like a moist breeze calming a fire, taking all of his anxieties away. He stared at the bottle, stunned, incredulous, and took another swallow. And another. And another.

An hour later he'd finished both six-packs. He'd never felt so good. He didn't feel drunk, or drugged; he felt *alive*, connected to everything, more aware of beauty and wonder than he'd ever been.

"What's gotten into you?" Brittney said when he came into the bedroom. She was already in bed with a book. He tore the book from her hands, ripped off both their shirts, and made love to her in a way that left them both happily dazed.

"Where did that come from?" she asked, snuggling up to him after.

"I don't know," he lied. But he did know.

He went back to Aram's every night for a week, always buying two six-packs of Scratch Ale, always getting the same effect. During the days he was more focused in his job hunting, and he secured several promising interviews with start-up tech firms.

Then came the night that he went to the beer section at Aram's, and the unthinkable happened: there was no Scratch Ale.

Aram saw him looking, called out from the front counter, "Sorry, my friend, but we sold out of that beer you like. Turns out a *lot* of people like it."

Dave felt panic rise up. "You're out of it?"

"Yeah, 'fraid so."

Heart racing, Dave asked, "Are you sure you don't maybe have some in the back…?"

Aram raised a finger. "You know, let me be sure. Hang on."

He stepped away for a second, went through a door behind the cooler sections, returned a few minutes later with two bottles adorned with the little scarlet imp. "I've got two singles left —"

Dave cut him off, pulling out his wallet, fingers shaking as he withdrew the bills. "I'll take 'em."

Fifteen minutes later he was at home with two empty bottles, and a desperate desire for more. Two bottles of bliss just weren't enough; he wanted — no, he needed — more.

He grabbed the car keys and drove to another liquor store. And another. And another.

By the end of the night he'd been to sixteen liquor stores. Twelve had never heard of either Scratch Ale or Lew's C4 Brewery. Three had carried the beer, but sold out. One had four six-packs left. Dave bought them all.

After he finished two of the six-packs, he pulled out his phone and started searching for Lew's C4 Brewery. If they were local, maybe he could buy direct from them.

He found nothing. No listing anywhere for them. He tried alternate spellings, the name of the brew itself, but…nothing.

Four nights went by, and Dave began to wonder if this was how junkies felt coming off heroin, except he had no physical side effects, just the all-consuming desperate yearning to experience that ecstasy again. It was all he thought about, all he wanted. He felt it in his head, his heart, his blood.

It occurred to him that maybe he could get the brewery's address from Aram, so he went to the store to ask. Aram smiled apologetically, said, "Sorry, my friend, I just bought it from a local distributor, not the actual brewery." He gave Dave the name of the distributor. When Dave called them the next day, they said they'd never heard of Lew's C4 Brewery.

Dave went back to Aram's that night. "Hey, you gave me the wrong distributor. They said they never heard of that brewery."

Aram scratched his beard. "That's strange, but that's the only distributor I buy from. I cannot explain that."

"I can," Dave said, feeling rage consume his desperate need, "You lied to me to keep it a secret for yourself." He turned around and marched out.

Last year, there'd been a rash of home invasions in their 'hood and Brittney had insisted on buying a handgun, "for defense." She kept it in her bedside table, loaded. Dave marched home, ignored her queries, went into the bedroom, withdrew it from her bedstand.

When he heard Brittney ask, "What are you doing with that?" from the bedroom doorway, he turned around and shot her. It was easier than trying to answer her pointless question.

Next, he returned to the liquor store and confronted Aram. When Aram saw the gun, he held up his hands, smiling that smile again. "Look, my friend, if I had the beer, I would give it to you –"

Dave wasn't interested in excuses, so he shot Aram.

He left the liquor store, intending to go back to his car and drive until he found somewhere that had Scratch Ale. In the parking lot, a man was looking up, shocked, a six-pack in his hand. Dave saw red imps grinning at him from the bottles, so he fired at the man, blowing out a large part of his head. The six-pack fell to the asphalt, shattering two precious bottles. Dave rushed forward to rescue the rest, but saw that what he'd mistaken for the imp was actually a bird, and the beer wasn't Scratch Ale.

"Sorry, my friend," he heard. He'd just barely looked back to see Aram, blood-stained but standing with a shotgun pointed at him. Aram pulled the trigger.

Dave came to in the lawn chair on his balcony. Disoriented, he looked around, saw the same dying plants, the same smoggy night overhead, the same cookie-cutter apartments around him. He heard clinking and realized the balcony was cluttered with empty bottles of Scratch Ale, dozens and dozens of them…

But he felt that mad itching, that terrible yearning for more of the stuff. It consumed him, leaving him wanting more than anything to scratch that itch. He began grabbing bottles, tilting them up, hoping for one last drop, but the bottles were bone-dry.

One of the imps winked at him. When he froze, staring, it laughed at him from the paper label. Once it got the raucous howls under control, it said, in a voice like metal grating on metal, "Oh, Dave, you're really a fuckin' idiot."

"Whaaa…huh?" he asked.

"You couldn't even figure out the brewery name, you moron."

"The brewery name…?"

"Say it out loud, Dave."

"Lew's C4 Brewery…" It hit him, then, like a punch right to the gut. "*Lucifer.*"

"Yep. And guess where you are now."

Confused, he scanned the surroundings before looking back at the talking imp on the beer bottle label. "On my balcony…"

The imp screeched laughter again. "Oh, baby, you just keep thinking that. How do you feel about now?"

"Like I'd give my soul for one more of those beers."

"Little late for that, dude."

As the imp continued to shriek, Dave started to shake with terror and that awful need. He knew where he was, he knew how long he'd be there, and he knew how he'd feel for the rest of f eternity.

ALL TRICKS

Brad stepped out of his house, walked to the sidewalk, clutched his empty pillowcase, and stopped to breathe in the Halloween smells: dead leaves, opened pumpkins, and something else...

Fear. That was his favorite scent.

It was just after eight, and the street still resounded with the shrieks and giggles of kids dressed as monsters, princesses, and superheroes. Brad smiled at a family that passed him; the two kids, dressed as a ninja and a mermaid, didn't even notice him; their parents frowned.

He didn't let that bother him, because tonight was his night. He'd always loved Halloween, that one night of the year when he was free to be someone else. When he was little, his mom had gone out with him, accompanying her pint-sized soldier or hobo or vampire as they traipsed from house to house. After his mom left (for good, without even a note or a final kiss), he'd gone out alone. It was still the one night when other kids didn't know who he was behind his mask, when they didn't laugh at his frayed, ill-fitting clothes and call him "Brad the Sad", when teachers didn't invite him to stay after class so they could hear his story about how the latest goose egg was because he was clumsy, he'd tripped, he'd accidentally walked into a door.

On Halloween he could be Brad the Bad.

He knew that at 15 he was too old to trick or treat; he also knew that his costume wasn't much – just a hoodie with the hood pulled up, which was how he usually wore it anyway. That made him stop and think: since it was Halloween, maybe he should push it back and let everyone see his bruised face. They'd probably think the black eye and purple nose were really good make-up.

Reaching up, Brad pulled the hoodie back and paused to consider his mission. He was no ordinary trick or treater, no kid out for candy and the praise of adults.

He knew that this night, when the gates between worlds opened, had brought demons to earth. Some of them were here, on his street.

Closing his eyes, Brad let his thoughts drift away as his senses focused, seeking out the nearest unearthly visitor. After a few seconds his eyes popped open; he was staring at the house of Mr. Bohringer, on the other side of the street three houses down.

That was where he'd start, then.

Brad's adrenaline began to ramp up as he crossed the street. Mr. Bohringer – Dean, to his friends – sometimes came over to drink beer with Dad. Since Mrs. Bohringer had died last year (lung cancer, thanks to her three-pack-a-day habit), Dean had hung out a lot more with Brad's father. Just last week they'd sat together in lawn chairs in the backyard, killing two six-packs. When Dad had slugged Brad in front of the neighbor for knocking over a half-full bottle, Mr. Bohringer had just looked away, said nothing.

Ever since Dad had knocked his son out with a piece of two-by-four last year, Brad's life had changed. He'd become aware of things he hadn't known about before; he could glimpse the things that moved in the shadows, he could hear them whisper to each other. He'd listened as they'd made plans for Halloween; now they were here, and he was the only one who knew.

Mr. Bohringer's lights were off; there was no cheerful, grimacing pumpkin glowing on his porch steps. The families walked by his house to the next, but Brad strode right up the front walk, pulled the tattered screen door back, and knocked loudly on the door. When there was no response, he pounded again.

The door was flung open and Mr. Bohringer stood framed there, his face twisted in rage. "What the fuck's wrong with –" He broke off as he saw Brad standing there. "Oh, it's you. What do you want, kid? Everything okay with your dad?"

Brad nodded, but when he tried to answer he found his throat suddenly too dry to form sounds, because he saw the demon hiding inside Mr. Bohringer's skin, wearing it like a cheap store-bought Halloween costume.

It was now or never.

Reaching into his pillowcase, Brad pulled out the kitchen knife he'd brought from home and drove it into the demon's chest.

The thing that was disguised as Mr. Bohringer gasped and fell back, clutching at the knife. As it tumbled to the floor, Brad watched, his heart beating so hard he thought his own chest might explode. He waited, stepping away from the blood that fountained up, feeling satisfaction as the demon convulsed and finally died. It was only then that he reached down, yanked the knife free and wiped the blood on Mr. Bohringer's shirt before returning the blade to his pillowcase. He hadn't done a very good job with the first demon of the night – some of his demon-Dad's blood had gotten on the white pillowcase – so he'd learned from that.

He walked away from Mr. Bohringer's house but paused in the street to watch two young pranksters hurl eggs at the dark windows before fleeing. Apparently Brad wasn't the only who knew about Mr. Bohringer. He wondered if any of the eggs might have hit the demon corpse, his second of the night, cooling in a pool of its own blood just inside the open front door.

The night is all tricks, Brad thought, smiling. Then he turned to the left, heading for the next demon. The night was young, and he had so much to do.

DOUBLE VISION

The acid-house band on the stage of the Pyramid Theater had just ripped into their third song when Ofelia looked into the crowd and saw herself.

At first she assumed she was looking into a mirror, but there was a wall sconce casting yellow light on the faded gold paneling that had been chic eighty years ago. What she saw was no reflection.

It was someone who resembled her, then…but the longer she watched, the more she realized the woman she was looking at didn't just have her same hair color (auburn), but was wearing exactly the same clothing – the black tee with the graphic of the flowering skull, the blue pants with the white stripe she'd found at the second-hand clothing store.

They were separated by about forty feet, and the interior of the Pyramid was dark, the lights focused on the stage, but Ofelia had seen the woman well enough to be stunned by the resemblance. Just last night her friend Tomas had been telling her about doppelgängers – mysterious doubles – and something about the Pyramid Theater, but Ofelia had been high and hadn't paid much attention to what he'd said. "Hey," she yelled over the music, turning to her friend Melly, "check that out…"

But her friend – who loved this band even though Ofelia thought they were just okay – was bouncing to the music; without taking her eyes from the stage, she shouted, "WHAT?"

The woman who looked like Ofelia saw her then. For a second their eyes locked, and Ofelia thought she saw alarm there; then the woman turned and began pushing through the throbbing crowd, heading for the nearest exit.

Ofelia's heart began to pound; she was filled with an inexplicable sense of dread, as if she'd just opened the front door of her apartment and saw an endless, impassable hole. "I'll be right back," she yelled at her friend. Melly gave no sign of hearing her.

Ofelia didn't immediately spot the other woman at first; then she saw her, slipping through the exit. Ofelia began rushing through the crowd, ignoring the curses and looks of those she stumbled into.

She made it through the exit a few seconds later, and stood at one end of the old art deco theater's lobby. To the left was the long concession stand; before her, a wide flight of stairs leading up to the balcony, and to her right, more stairs down to the basement. *There* – she just got a glimpse of a dark red head descending. She strode to the basement stairs and ran down, her feet moving as quickly as the dancers' in the theater.

At the bottom of the stairs, she stood at one end of the basement, the walls covered in gaudy hieroglyphic-themed wallpaper that dated back to the 1930s. Benches lined the walls; signs pointed to the restrooms. The music from above thudded, creating a soundquake. The space was empty.

Ofelia heard a door closing and ran forward, following the sound. She thought it came from the hallway that led to the women's bathroom. She turned the corner and saw a long corridor before her; the swinging door into the restroom was to the right, and Ofelia pushed through it.

She knew instantly, with that uncanny sense of detection that all humans possess to some extent, that she was alone here. She still moved along the row of stalls, pushing on doors, until she reached the last one.

Empty.

Where could the other woman have gone?

Ofelia turned to exit the bathroom when she glanced to her right – and felt her heart stop.

She stood in front of a long line of sinks, a mirror mounted above them...an *empty mirror*. Ofelia was not reflected in it. There were the sinks, the stalls behind her...but not her. She waved her arms, moved closer, but her reflection was simply not there, not even a transparent shape or outline. It was as if she'd ceased to exist beyond the mirror.

As she stood paralyzed, staring, the main door in the reflection opened, but she heard nothing. Glancing to the side, she saw the door to the bathroom – her bathroom – hadn't moved.

In the mirror, she entered the bathroom, walked forward until she stood directly opposite Ofelia, and then the reflection froze, just as she had frozen.

Ofelia opened her mouth to say something, then stopped, realizing how ridiculous that would be – was she actually going to try to talk to her *reflection?* She saw the mirror Ofelia's mouth twist, mimicking hers.

She suddenly felt as if she was the victim of some incredibly complex practical joke; anger boiled up in her, and she shouted, "Stop it!"

Mirror Ofelia shouted, too, but without sound.

"I saw you, you know," she said.

For a second, Ofelia thought she saw fear cross her double's face, but then she wondered – wasn't she afraid, and wasn't that just the mirror image of her own fear?

"Fuck," she muttered. She couldn't be sure of anything.

Ofelia mentally re-traced her steps, looking for something she'd missed. The concert…the first sighting of the double…following her down the stairs…losing her in the hallway outside the bathroom – *That was it.*

Ofelia rushed to the door and looked to the end of the hallway. There, to the right, under a single dim light – another door, completely unmarked. It didn't look like any other door she'd seen in the theater; it was wooden, dark, with an ancient-looking doorknob. She turned the knob, realized the door wasn't locked. Taking a deep breath, Ofelia readied herself, pulled the door open –

At first Ofelia thought the door opened onto a mirror, because what she saw was herself standing in the hallway – but when she thrust out one hand, there was no polished surface. The other Ofelia stumbled back to avoid the touch.

"You shouldn't be here!" said the doppelgänger.

Ofelia stared, trying to figure out what was wrong with the other version of her, and she finally realized: it was a mirror image of her, with everything reversed. On her right shoulder, Ofelia had a tattoo with a cherub and the name of her brother, Duff, who'd died in a car accident last year. She pulled her sleeve up and turned her right arm to the double. The other Ofelia copied the action, and Ofelia saw that the tattoo was there, reading F-F-U-D.

Reversed.

Terrified, Ofelia barely got out, "What's going on? Why do you look like me?"

"Because," the other answered, "I am you. I'm you in this world, and you –" she pointed behind Ofelia, "–are me in that world."

"But you were…"

The double cut off. "I know – I was in your world. I don't think this is supposed to happen, but I heard about the door…" She gestured at the aged wood portal.

Ofelia looked at the door, feeling its power and age, and asked, her voice soft, "Why is it *here?*"

"It moves all the time. My friend Tomas told me about it –"

Ofelia's heart skipped a beat, as she remembered more of the stoned conversation with *her* friend Tomas. "Last night, Tomas was talking about doppelgängers, doubles, and said he'd heard about this door in the basement of the Pyramid Theater. I was going to come down here and look at it for him…"

"Of course you were," said the doppelgänger. "I just did it first. And then I saw *you*, and I kind of freaked out. I'm not sure if it's safe for us to meet or not."

The air around them began to tremble; Ofelia felt massive energy building around her. She looked back and saw the door slowly swinging shut. She cried out, just as the doppelgänger did. "You need to go back while the door's still open!"

Ofelia didn't think; she leaped. The world imploded, deafening and crushing her. She crumpled, but didn't lose consciousness. She saw the world waiver for a few seconds before it settled back into solid reality.

Panting, she sat up, almost too scared to look…but finally she did, and saw that the ancient door had vanished. Where it had been was now nothing but a wall, covered in the same vintage hieroglyphic wallpaper that the rest of the Pyramid Theater was.

She felt safe, but there was one last test to be made. Still trembling, she made her way back to the restroom, pushed through the door, and went to the mirror.

Her reflection was there, looking as pale and frightened as she was, copying her movements perfectly. Relief flooded through Ofelia.

She knew she'd never take her mirror image for granted again.

TOIL AND TROUBLE

As Astrid finished the invocation to open the séance, she wondered if the demon Chort might appear.

Chort had plagued her for the last two years, ever since she'd tricked the demon into releasing her friend Abel's soul after he'd drunkenly lost it during a poker match in Vegas. The demon had taken the form of a handsome young gambler, plied Abel with martinis until he'd jokingly agreed to wager his soul, and then been identified by Astrid when she'd summoned a breeze to knock off his hat and had spotted the stubby horns in his black hair. She'd promptly challenged the demon to a final hand, called down some favors from the spirits, and laid out a royal flush to regain Abel's soul. The next day Abel, head throbbing from his hangover, remembered none of it.

Since then, Chort – who had realized she was a powerful witch as soon as she'd laid down her cards – had messed with her at every opportunity. He caused herbs to die in her garden. He blew out the candles during rituals. He'd shredded her favorite black lace shawl. He'd even bitten one client on the ankle as Astrid had cleared her house with white sage. He was a trickster demon and unlikely to be lethal, but Astrid knew that his pranks would only grow worse.

She hoped he wouldn't be here tonight, because this was an important event for her. She'd been called in by Jasper Axton, the handsome paranormal superstar and creator of the long-running reality series *Ghost Talking*, to lead a séance in an episode filmed in Santa Mira's Goldrush Inn, said to be the most haunted building on the west coast. At 50, Astrid had almost given up ever getting on *Ghost Talking*, even though the camera still loved her thick blond hair and warm, generous features, so when the show's producer had called she'd been ecstatic. The timing was perfect: Astrid's new book, *Magick Life*, could use a boost in sales – even a witch had bills to pay – and an appearance on *Ghost Talking* would be sure to provide one.

As long as Chort didn't show up with a monkey wrench or two. She'd secretly gone to the Inn a day early to lay down a few protection spells which she hoped would keep the demon out, but he was a mischievous monster with centuries of experience.

Astrid finished calling on the elemental spirits, and immediately felt the atmosphere in the third floor suite change. The suite, which had been kept with its original nineteenth-century furnishings and was said to be the most active room in the inn, suddenly felt crowded with the unseen, all jostling to be heard.

Astrid breathed in deeply and smiled. "Ahh," she said, half-glimpsing the cameras positioned around the room capturing this for the television audience, "there are so many of you here!" She turned on her spirit box, which began to sound a rush of white noise. "Would anyone like to tell us their name?"

There was a second before the box blurted out, "Jesse."

The three men, including Jasper, and two women seated with Astrid at the table all looked at each other, eager, excited. Astrid continued. "Hello, Jesse. Thank you for talking with us. Is there anything you'd like to say?"

The spirit box pulsed more static before saying what sounded like, "Danger."

Jasper – known for his well-timed dramatic asides – stage-whispered, "Did you hear that?"

One of his assistants, a tall bear of a man named Scott, answered, "Was that 'danger'?"

Astrid ignored them to focus on the spirit. "Jesse, who's in danger?"

The spirit box answered, clearly, *"All of you."*

Astrid felt the first stirrings of unease. Was this Chort? If so, it might be a trick that would backfire, because Jasper's expressive, bearded face was lighting up with the promise of ratings.

A pretty young woman with a pixie haircut and a tattoo sleeve of skeletons abruptly gasped. "Holy crap, my K-2 just went nuts!" They all glanced at the meter on the table before her, which had just shot from a green light all the way to the red at the right. The needle jittered there but didn't drop back down. All eyes turned to the dim corners of the large space.

Scott cried out, "There!" He pointed at a spot on the wall near the old brick fireplace.

"What?" Jasper asked, following his gaze.

"I saw something – a shadow figure."

A loud bang sounded from the wall.

Someone at the table murmured, "*Oh fuck…*" Astrid knew they'd bleep that in post.

A series of bangs, ten in all, sounded, followed by a distant laughter.

Scott, his face pale, was out of his chair. "This is too weird, man, I'm outta here –"

Jasper caught his wrist and held on. "Sit down, Scott. We're safe…aren't we, Astrid?"

"Yes. We've each been blessed with protection." But behind her calm and charismatic exterior, she wasn't so sure. When spirits got this physical, it might mean they were not spirits at all; they could be elementals, or demons that might be worse than Chort. She closed her eyes, inhaled deeply, and tried to open herself to whatever was in the room with them…

There were the dead, anxious to commune with the living, some of them angry, some just lonely; there were the others around the table, their energy warm…but there was something else, too, something not exactly malevolent, something…*human.*

Astrid stood abruptly, ignoring the shouted questions from Jasper and the cameramen, and strode to a closed door in the corner where the sounds had emanated from. She flung the door open, reached in for a light switch, and saw a man in the room, his right hand still raised to pound on the wall.

The man stared at her, caught in the act; Astrid turned away from him and called out to Jasper, "This had better not be one of your crew, Jasper, because you promised no bullshit."

Jasper leapt up from the table and ran to join her, gaping at the cowering young man in wire-frame glasses and knit cap. "I don't know this clown," he said. "Who the fuck are you?"

The man was trembling now. "I…my girlfriend's on the staff here at the inn, and I just thought…"

From somewhere in the room, a director shouted, "CUT!" Astrid heard a hubbub behind her, as angry crewmembers argued with each other about who'd fallen down on the job.

Astrid, however, was concentrating now on something new assaulting her senses – the energy in this room felt wrong. She stared at the young man, still babbling about how he'd only wanted to have a little fun, and then she looked at him again and knew:

The knit cap.

She reached out and yanked it away as the young man cried out and pulled back while Jasper watched, perplexed. Astrid followed him as he backed into a corner, holding his hands over his head. She grabbed one and pulled it down while Jasper shouted, "Astrid, what –"

There were the horns. Astrid dropped the wrist and said, "Hello, Chort. I wondered when you'd show up."

Jasper asked, "Who is Chort?"

"A shapeshifting trickster Slavic demon who's been following me for the last two years."

Without dropping a beat, Jasper waved the nearest cameraman over and pointed at Chort.

Astrid faced the demon, laughing at him. "Did you think this form would fool me?"

"It almost did, witch."

Reaching into a pocket, Astrid brought out the elaborate Russian Orthodox crucifix with its three crossbeams that her Book of Shadows said would work against Chort. "Show yourself," she said as she thrust the crucifix forward.

The slender young man with curly hair and glasses morphed in a single eyeblink into a small demon with dark gray skin, legs that bent backwards and ended in hooves, red eyes and short black horns. The demon flinched at the sight of the crucifix, holding up one hand to shield himself. "Damn you," he said, in a guttural voice.

Astrid stepped forward, pushing the sacred object ever closer to the demon, who crouched in a corner, unable to retreat further. "Ya know something, Chort? I'm sick and tired of you always getting in my shit. Leave me alone, or I'm gonna cram this crucifix right down your throat, and that is not gonna feel good."

The demon waved its hands frantically. "Okay, I got it! I'll back down. I'm done." There was a bright flash and Chort vanished.

Jasper turned to the cameraman. "Tell me you got that."

The cameraman, his voice trembling, answered, "I got that."

Jasper turned to Astrid. "That was the most incredible thing I've ever seen." He held up a hand to high-five her, but Astrid was suddenly exhausted, her energy completely drained by the encounter with the demon.

"I need to sleep," was all she said.

As she fell back on the bed in the room, her last thought was to hope the publishers would be able to keep up with demand for her book once this aired.

DARK RIDE

As Dani and Evan walked through the county fairgrounds looking for the haunted house ride, she risked a side glance at him and thought, *He's actually not too bad.*

They'd met via an online dating service, where Dani had included her love of dark rides ("the older and cheesier, the better!") in her profile. Evan's had also mentioned dark rides ("If you like to get scared in a ride, I'm your guy"), they'd texted, and, since it was late summer, arranged a date at the County Fair.

It was a Friday night, and although the area just beyond the front entrance was crowded with strolling families and couples clutching cotton candy and corn dogs, the haunted house ride was situated away from the action, at the fairgrounds' far edge. Evan bought them tickets and then led the way. As they walked, they made the usual small talk: traffic, work, weather.

He doesn't seem TOO creepy, Dani thought.

"So have you always loved dark rides?" he asked, as they strolled the midway, between game and food stalls.

"Yeah, but it's a little more than that. I'm part of a group that's putting together a study of them. We go to as many as we can, catalog them, stuff like that."

"Wow. So you've got almost a professional interest."

"Almost."

"How many have you personally been to?"

Dani took a second to calculate before she answered, "Thirty-six."

Finally they found the haunted house ride, set apart from the midway, appropriately – eerily – isolated. There were only two couples in line before them as Dani and Evan walked up the ramp to the boarding area.

"I love that stupid mural," Dani said, eyeing the grotesque, badly-painted monsters adorning the ride's façade. Jagged letters in yellow shrieked "HAUNTED HOUSE" above portraits of a vampire, a zombie, and several things that were simply unidentifiable. Dani paused to photograph it before putting her phone back in her shoulder bag.

Evan smiled as he took it in the cheap art. "It's pretty great, in that so-bad-it's-good way."

Dani had to admit he was kind of cute, in a nerdy, fanboy way. He wore a beat-up old leather jacket that he probably thought was either hip or hid his chunkiness, but she guessed it was a hand-me-down from an older brother.

One of the couples before them boarded. The ride attendant, a tall, gangly dude with long stringy hair wearing overalls, didn't seem to be in any hurry.

"What all do you carry in that huge thing?" Evan asked, nodding at the colorful knit bag she had slung over her shoulder.

"Oh," Dani said, looking down, "the usual girl stuff: phone, tissues, hand sanitizer, mace."

Evan's eyebrows went up. "Mace? In case the date didn't work out?"

"Or for the monsters in this terrifying haunted house," Dani said, trying to sound cheerful.

The last couple before them climbed into a clanking car that squealed as it rounded the first curve and bumped through the wooden doors going into the ride. From inside, Dani heard the sounds of recorded demonic laughter, screams, and hydraulic blasts.

"We're up next," Evan said. He reached out and took her hand. She let him. His grip was nice: firm without crushing, dry and gentle.

Finally they were the last couple in line; no one else had come up to wait behind them. The lanky attendant let a few cars go by empty before he waved them up. "What was he waiting for?" Dani whispered as they were seated in the old rickety wooden car.

"Maybe to let stuff reset," Evan whispered back.

Silently, the attendant pulled the safety bar down over them, then punched a button on a control board beside the track. The car shot forward, moving toward the first door. "Here we go," Evan muttered as he gave her hand a little squeeze.

Once inside, the sensations began: there, as usual with dark rides, were the strobing lights catching horrific figures and painted walls, there were the sounds of whooping laughter and, from somewhere farther down the track, ominous organ music…but there was something else in this ride, something different: a bad smell, like food that had been rotting for a long time.

A giant rat, its fake fur matted with age, shot forward at them, its air ram an amplified hiss. Evan laughed before leaning in close. "Hey, did you know there's an urban legend about this dark ride?"

"No," Dani said, her eyes riveted to a tunnel that now swirled madly around the car, its colorful sides illuminated in blacklight. "What is it?"

"They say that some of the figures in this ride are real."

"Real? Like, what – real werewolves?"

"No. Like…" The car turned a corner, its wheels squealing, banged through a door painted like a stone castle wall, and wound its way down a corridor lined with hanging bodies. "Like *those*. Real."

Dani looked up and had to admit that the overhead figures were better than the average dark ride mannequins; their flesh was impressively withered and darkened, the hair scraggly, lips drawn back to reveal brown teeth. But more than the visuals, Dani noticed that smell again, the smell of something gone bad. She knew about the scent cannons that were used in the major amusement park haunted mazes, but was surprised that a cheap carnival dark ride had something that sophisticated.

"But they're just dummies," she said.

"Are you sure?"

She actually *wasn't*. As the car rumbled on, she counted ten of the hanged figures, all displaying the same attention to gruesome detail.

They reached the end of that section, the car swerved, pounded through another set of doors, and…

The new scene was a graveyard, filled with cheap cardboard cut-out tombstones sporting ludicrous names like "Sam E. Terry", lit in flashing deep blue light that imprinted the images on Dani's retinas.

And there were more bodies, thrown down on graves, spilling out of plywood coffins, propped up against the walls.

The car reached the middle of the graveyard scene and rattled to a halt.

Dani looked around. "Why have we stopped?" She started to pull her hand away from her date's, but his grip tightened on her wrist. "Evan…?"

"I didn't get to tell you the rest of the urban legend about this place: they say it's owned by this clan who have a bunch of dark rides like this one, that they occasionally kill the guests, use some of the victims for props, but eat the rest." He let his eyes pass over her before adding, "Guess which one you're gonna be?"

His other hand reached under that stupid leather jacket and came out holding something that made a little thwick sound as he pressed a button. Dani caught the sudden gleam of a blade under the flickering blue light. He drew his arm back, pulled her closer, grinned –

She fired her pistol right through the bag, and Evan took two bullets to the chest and one to the right thigh. The impact threw him out of the car onto one of the coffins. He clutched weakly at his wounds, blood gushing through his fingers as he looked up at her in shock and confusion.

"You dumbshit," Dani said, as she stepped out of the car, her ears still ringing from the shots. "You had me until you launched into the 'urban legend' bullshit. If it hadn't been for that, you might've taken me by surprise. As it is, now I'm going to go hunt down the rest of your little cannibal clan and take them out. Thanks for making it easy." When her keys fell out of the fresh holes in the bag, Dani kicked Evan angrily. "Damn, now I have to get a new bag, asshole."

Evan convulsed a last time and then went still. As Dani wound up the ruined bag and tucked it under one arm, she knew she might not have much time to finish the job. She hoped the rest of the family wasn't armed; that always made it harder. And she still had so much work to do.

After all, there were dark rides in carnivals and fairs and amusement parks all over the world.

THE CITY'S
SECRET HEART

"Are you ready for tonight?"

Nessa juggled her phone with one hand and her make-up with the other. "Almost," she told Skye as she finished applying eyeliner.

On the phone, Skye said, "I'll be there in ten, okay?"

"Meet you out front."

Nessa finished the call and her makeup, took one last look in the mirror, and tried not to be too critical. She wanted to look good for tonight, even though she didn't know exactly what she'd be doing.

That was one of the great things about the Secret City Society: when you got the text with nothing but a time and a place, you never knew what it would lead to. Skye had found out about the Society from an ex who had invited her in, and when they'd broken up she'd asked Nessa to come with her. That first trip had been a visit to a secret night market that dealt in curiosities; Nessa had left with a vase made from glass encasing butterfly wings. The next invitation had come a week later, and had taken the two friends to a party held in an abandoned movie palace where they'd been served absinthe as they watched live fire-eaters and contortionists perform.

Nessa felt strangely at home with the six other members of the Secret City Society. Even though Skye was the only one she saw outside of the events, she felt comfortable on the outings, no matter how bizarre they were. She'd never really felt like she belonged anywhere else; she'd always been on the outside looking in. Sometimes Nessa had felt different because of things she *guessed*, like she thought there was a secret life to her city that she would only need to find the key to open.

The Secret City Society was the key, the city had opened its wonders to her, and she'd found her place at last.

She lived for the texts that arrived on her phone. Tonight: *4th St. downtown subway stop, 10 p.m.*, it might say. She'd look up from her office desk, already feeling the thrum of excitement, so intense she was almost surprised her co-workers didn't sense it.

Part of belonging to the SCS, though, was that she couldn't tell anyone about it. She couldn't snap a selfie at the demonstration of musical instruments made entirely from bones and post it on social media; she couldn't text other friends and tell them that she'd just watched a man in a prototype jet pack take off from the roof of a ship docked near Catalina. When Skye had first invited her to join the SCS, she'd told Nessa that she believed some of the members monitored social media platforms to make sure everyone stayed quiet.

Nessa was happy to follow that rule. She liked having hidden knowledge that couldn't be shared.

Tonight, though, promised to be really special. Skye had told her that Nessa had duly impressed some of the other members, and they thought she was ready for "the next step." Nessa had no idea what that meant, but she wanted it.

She met Skye outside and climbed into her friend's Prius. Skye eyed her and nodded, "Ohh, girlfriend, you are smoking. Love that new hair color." Nessa had found a violet she'd liked and was wearing it for the first time tonight; she was relieved when Skye complimented it. "Thanks."

Today's text had provided only an address and a time (11 p.m.). The address was on the city's eastern edge.

"Did you google the address?" Nessa asked.

"No – I'm just following the directions now. Why?"

"Because I think it's a cemetery."

Skye shot a look at her friend. "Okay. That's pretty cool."

Nessa giggled before agreeing. "It is."

They chattered about the usual things on the drive; it was late enough that traffic was light, Skye always drove fast, and they were there twenty minutes later. As Skye's GPS directions ended, they both looked up to see two huge stone columns supporting a sign that read, "Hillview Cemetery."

"You were right," Skye said, peering out the windshield. "Do we go in, or…?"

The main gates were locked, but there was a smaller side entrance that had a sign taped to it reading only SCS. "I think that little gate is open."

Skye found a spot on the street, parked, and they walked to the open gate. As they neared it, Nessa saw a man waiting just inside, mostly in shadow. He stepped forward into the light, and she was relieved to see it was Justin, one of the other SCS members. "Hey, you two," he called in greeting, opening the gate for them.

They stepped through, and Nessa turned to watch as he locked the door behind them with a heavy chain. "Are we the last to arrive?" she asked.

"Yep. This way." He walked before them, leaving them to follow. Nessa swallowed down a small surge of unease at being locked inside the cemetery, reasoning that it was more to keep intruders out than to cage them in.

As they walked through the cemetery, the outside world seemed to vanish: a tall brick wall shut out both the sight and sound of the surrounding urban neighborhood. The cemetery was dark, with only the occasional overhead light; either Justin's memory or his night vision was extraordinary, since he led the way without extra illumination. When Skye stumbled, she pulled out her phone to use as a flashlight.

"Damn, Justin," Skye said, "how can you see anything?"

Justin didn't answer.

They walked in silence for a few seconds, and then Skye leaned close to Nessa to say, "I feel kind of like I'm in a horror movie."

Nessa responded, "Wouldn't it be cool if that's what we're going to do tonight – making a horror movie in a real cemetery?"

The grounds were old and not incredibly well kept, which made the whole place both moody and tragic. The grass was yellow and overgrown, tombstones and monuments were cracked and tilting, the trees leafless and likely dying.

They finally saw a small ring of lights ahead. "There they are," Skye said, her relief obvious.

Nessa asked, "So maybe a séance…?"

Skye shrugged. "We'll find out."

They met up with the six other current members of the Secret City Society. In addition to the taciturn Justin, there was Jasmine, beautiful and cynical, the leader; Marshall, the academic with button-down shirt and a perpetual book bag slung over one shoulder; Tanya, the diminutive actress who seemed always on the brink of stardom; Phil, in his fifties, an aerospace engineer; and Luis, the second-newest member, who was shy and cute and who Nessa desperately wanted to work up the courage to ask about his orientation.

The other members greeted them as they approached, then Jasmine said, "We're all here now, so I guess we can get started."

The group fell silent as Jasmine moved about lighting candles that Nessa only now noticed. When she was done, she said, "Skye, if you'd put your phone away…"

"Oh, sorry." Skye turned it off and shoved it in her bag.

Jasmine took a deep breath, held it, exhaled, and grinned. "Let's do it."

"All right!" cried out Phil, as he unbuttoned his shirt.

"Uh," Nessa said, watching in confusion as the others either undressed or trembled, "what –"

She broke off as Phil's face abruptly lengthened, his nose and jaws turning into a fanged snout, back hunching, a howl escaping his furred throat.

Beside him, Tanya grew six more legs and began to crawl. Justin's dark skin turned ashen gray as his fingers hooked into claws, his teeth growing so much that they bloodied his own lips. Marshall simply faded away, but his book bag stayed suspended, and it took Nessa a few moments to realize that he'd become invisible. Jasmine's hair transformed into venomous, hissing snakes as her skin turned scaly and the color of brackish water. And Luis, sweet Luis, sloughed off both clothing and skin to become a living skeleton, his bones clacking like percussion instruments with every movement.

Nessa staggered back, stunned, before turning to her friend. "Skye –"

Skye's eyes were glowing golden, soft fur replacing her skin, a tail sprouting from her back as she fell to all fours.

Jasmine stepped up to Nessa, the snakes writhing and darting forward; when Nessa stumbled back, Jasmine laughed. "This," she said, gesturing at the others, "is our ultimate secret."

"You're all…" Nessa looked from one to the other of them before spitting out, "…monsters?"

"Yes," Skye said, winding around Nessa's legs. "This is who we really are."

Tanya, her voice high and breathy, added, "You've done a good job of keeping our secrets, Nessa. You passed the tests, so you're here tonight."

Nessa thought then, about how the Secret City Society had made her feel at home, welcomed, as if she truly belonged… did she belong? Was that really why she was here tonight? She searched inside herself for something, some essential part pushed down and buried for so long…but she couldn't find it.

She looked up at Jasmine and the rest for a clue. "Am…am I a monster, too?"

Somebody laughed, and the sound came out like a blade on a chalkboard. Jasmine eyed her for a moment with a mix of pity and scorn before saying, "Oh, no no no, baby – you're *dinner*."

As they moved forward, shrieking and groaning in hunger, Nessa could only hope they'd make it quick.

ON A MIST-SHROUDED SEA

Joey stared out at the featureless gray water surrounding his boat, a flat surface met at a near horizon by a wall of blank white mist. The *Sea Siren* bobbed gently beneath him, but it felt like the quiet before the storm.

He looked at his four passengers – three adult men all intent on their fishing rods and the one eight-year-old watching them with soft boredom – and knew they didn't feel the disquiet, but it wound its tendrils around Joey, tightening his anxiety.

He shouldn't have come out today – on the anniversary of Maggie's death – but George Rasalyan was a good client, and he'd offered to pay more than the usual fee for Joey to take him out today. His two older sons, Reynauld and Steve, were visiting from out of town, and it was a chance for them to all bond over one of the oldest of male rituals: fishing. George's youngest, Max, was too small to wield one of the heavy rods equipped for catching steelhead salmon, but he enjoyed watching his dad and brothers whenever a fish was on one of their lines.

Looking up at the curtain of mist, Joey couldn't even guess where the sun was. The forecast for today had mentioned a late afternoon storm coming in, but that was still hours away.

The weather had been like this a year ago, too…and then the storm had hit from out of nowhere. They'd had a newbie onboard that day whose line had continually snagged, and Maggie had been helping him when the wave had hit. The last Joey saw of his wife was when she'd been flipped overboard and tugged beneath the undulating surface. He rushed to the side of the boat, panicked, struggling to hang on in the wild water; he even nearly drowned diving in after her, but there was nothing. No trace of her had ever been found.

"Hey, are there pirates out here?"

Startled out of his bad memories, Joey looked down to see Max standing beside him, munching on a candy bar. The kid was cute, with dark curly hair and serious eyes but mischievous dimples; Maggie would've loved him. She'd loved kids almost as much as she loved the sea. In another year they might've had a child of their own, if the sea hadn't betrayed her…

He cut that thought off and instead answered Max, affecting a thick pirate dialect. "Arrggh, matey, there'd be only us."

Gazing out at the ocean, Max asked, "What about mermaids?"

Joey had to smile at that one. "Well…maybe, although I've never seen one."

"What about ghosts?"

That question sent a stab of alarm through Joey. "Ghosts? Why?"

Max shrugged, took another bite of chocolate. "I like ghosts."

Joey relaxed, remembering that the boy was eight; it was the kind of thing eight-year-olds asked, not a question burdened with extra meaning.

"So this is your boat?"

Nodding, Joey replied, "Yep."

"How does it work?"

"Well, I'll tell you what…" Joey glanced at the fish finder screen mounted above the throttle, saw no indications of fish, and decided to move. "How about if I let you take command so we can move to a better spot?"

The boy's eyes widened. "Really?" He rushed over to his father. "Dad, the captain says I can drive the boat!"

His father glanced back at Joey and grinned, then patted his son on the shoulder. "Atta boy!" George raised his eyes to Joey as he asked, "Should we reel in?"

"I think –" Joey broke off as some motion caught his peripheral vision. "Hang on…" The small color screen of the fish finder was suddenly showing a large block of shapes below them. "Looks like we're coming into some fish right here. Keep those lines out. We're going to trawl a little."

Max looked up excitedly. "Are we moving?"

"Just a little." Joey bent over, picked Max up, and sat him in the command chair. "You're in charge now, Max! We're going to ease the throttle forward just a little…"

For the next ten minutes, Joey showed the boy how to use the throttle to control the boat's engines and how to steer to follow the fish finder. Max was smart and took to it instantly.

"You're a natural," Joey told him, causing Max to beam.

George's oldest, twenty-two-year-old Reynauld, cried out as his rod bent. "I got one!"

He began reeling, his brawny arms bulging as he pulled back on the rod.

"That's a big one," George exclaimed.

"Yeah," Joey added, "don't reel too fast – just steady –"

"Hey, Cap'n Joey?" That was Max, still in the high seat.

Joey kept his eye on Reynauld's line as he grabbed the net and called back over his shoulder, "Yeah, Max?"

"There's something on the fish finder…"

"I can't look right now."

"But I think it's BIG."

Something thumped the bottom of the boat.

"Is that mine?" Reynauld said, pausing in his furious reeling.

"No," Joey answered, "keep pulling that line in."

The almost-electric buzzing sound of the cranking reel resumed.

Another *bang* sounded from the boat's hull.

George forgot about his line as his eyes scanned the water. "What is that – a whale?"

"Maybe…hey, everybody, let's all reel in."

George and his other son, Steve, began cranking in their lines. Reynauld kept fighting – and then his line abruptly went slack, his rod springing up. "Shit – I think I lost it."

The boat was hit again, this time strong enough to raise it out of the water on one side.

This had never happened to Joey before; alarm, colder than the surrounding mist, settled into his gut. He moved Max out of the chair, rushed to the stern of the boat to settle all three rods into their holders, and then called out, "Everybody hang on – we're getting out of here."

He ran back to the controls, grabbed the throttle, pushed it forward. The boat's engine roared, it began to move –

It hit something, hard.

"What *is* that?" one of the other men asked.

Joey didn't answer; he was too busy shifting into reverse, backing the *Sea Siren* away from whatever was out there…whatever was attacking it.

He spun the wheel as the boat slowed, stopped reversing –

A huge shape splashed out of the water to the port side. The men cried out and crouched in the boat. Max shouted, "A mermaid!"

Joey had only caught the leap in his peripheral vision. It had to have been a seal, or maybe a small whale –

It leapt again, this time on the other side. Joey was already looking in that direction, and he saw it this time: it was almost the color of the sea, a glinting gray, with a fishlike body, but the top part…even though it faded into the mist, he thought he could make out a shape like a woman's face.

A mermaid, in other words. Or maybe a ghost.

Joey blinked, stared harder, gaped, not because he'd seen a mermaid, but because he'd seen a mermaid whose face he knew so well, even half-hidden: it was Maggie's.

"See? A mermaid," Max said, beside Joey.

Joey nodded. "You were right."

The shape in the ocean sank below the surface.

The *Sea Siren's* engine idled, churning slate-hued water as Joey wiped at his wet eyes. He stumbled to the edge of the boat and looked down to see the big shape moving just below, circling the boat. He paid no attention to the screams of the three other men.

The mermaid – the ghost? – rose out of the water, balancing on its tail, to look at Joey. He saw sorrow there, and regret; he knew then why his wife's body had never been found. Somehow she'd changed, or been reborn, or blended, or come back as something less real…

Maybe, he thought, *mermaids were always just ghosts of those who died at sea.*

But he didn't really know, and it didn't matter, because what he also saw in its face – in her face – was invitation.

Joey drew his sleeve across his eyes and turned to the little boy behind him. "Max, do you think you can take this boat back to shore?"

Without opening his mouth, the boy nodded.

"Go slow until you're out of the mist, okay? You don't want to run into any other boats. But don't go too slow – there's a storm coming."

Max asked, "Where are you going?"

Joey gave him a final, fond look. He didn't even glance at the others. He saw only Maggie now.

He jumped into the sea.

HAZEL

What just happened? Where am I? Why can't I feel anything, or...

How did I get here, wherever "here" is? Remember...focus on that...

Brytny.

That's right – the girl I was dating. The one I met after I swiped right on the app. Her photo was gorgeous, and that first time we got together for coffee, I was happy to see she lived up to it. That was just a week ago…I think.

We chatted for two hours that night. She told me about her job, about how she was assistant to a development executive for a television production company, and how many guys she'd dated who really just wanted to use her to get to her boss. I told her about how I was moving up the ladder in a large health care firm. I didn't bother to mention that I made twenty-one dollars an hour and spent most of my days on a phone with irate patients. It wasn't like I was trying to marry this woman, after all. I just wanted to get her into bed.

Brytny raised only one alarm bell during that initial chat: she was into a lot of woo-woo ghost shit. I mean, really into it, as she owned equipment and went on ghost hunts and played me recordings of white noise that she claimed were her Uncle Bill calling to her from beyond the grave.

Me, I'm a man of science and facts. I don't believe in ghosts, magic, life after death, conspiracy theories, or any of that other nonsense. I believe in what's real, what's verifiable…what I can touch.

Especially that last part.

After that first date, we spent a week texting. Brytny sent me more ghost photos that I thought looked like she needed a new camera, but I told her they were really impressive.

She suggested we take a day trip. She'd just heard about a little town that was a three-hour drive to the north that had a museum that was supposed to be haunted. Or, rather, there was a specific object in the museum that was haunted: a doll. It was named Hazel, and although it had been in the museum for fifty years, it'd just been the subject of one of those ghost-hunting reality tv shows, and everyone wanted to see it now, including Brytny.

I agreed we should go, not because I was interested in some old toy, but because I was hoping once we were there, had toured the museum, had a nice lunch with a few glasses of wine, and were looking at a three-hour drive back, Brytny just might see the wisdom of spending the night there.

We made our plans to leave early Saturday morning. We'd be there by noon.

It all went fine at first. We had a nice drive out of the city, through the hills, past the farmlands, and into rural country that had once been home to pioneers and prospectors. We found the little town and the museum. Because of the tv show, it was a bit crowded but nothing awful.

The museum was in an old schoolhouse and full of crap like rusty gold pans and tattered dresses and moldy books. It wasn't big, just a single room, and the doll was easy to spot. It stood by itself in a glass cube on top of a table, a little handwritten card below it reading, "Hazel. Porcelain doll from 1892."

"There she is," Brytny whispered, as we entered the museum and spotted the doll right away. Brytny's eyes lit up. I hoped to make her light up for other reasons in a few hours; in the meantime, I could endure this, as silly as it was.

There were a few people gathered around the doll, taking selfies with it, talking in hushed tones. Brytny waited until they finished and walked away so we could have Hazel all to ourselves.

As Brytny stepped up to the table, she said, "Did you watch the episode of *Ghost Encounters* that featured her?"

I actually had, although I'd laughed and rolled my eyes. "Of course."

I had to admit there was something disturbing about the doll. It was ancient, of course, with its porcelain face cracking in fine lines like veins and its hair in tight ringlets; it was the eyes, though, that were the worst part – they really did seem to watch everything.

Brytny shivered. "Oooh, I can feel her – it's so heavy right around this table, like you're underwater." I felt nothing, but of course I wasn't a "sensitive" like Brytny claimed to be.

"So," I said, remembering the tv show, "what was that thing they said you should never do around this doll?"

"They said you should never be mean to her, like insult her or something. They had that footage of the one guy who did it, and he just keeled over right there."

"Do you actually believe that?"

Brytny turned to look at me. "I don't know, but I don't see any reason to do it, either."

She saw the smile on my face and frowned. "Matt, don't."

"C'mon – pull out your phone. We'll make a video and it'll go viral."

She didn't reach for her bag. "I'm serious – don't do it."

Now she was pissing me off. Nobody tells me what to do, especially not some airheaded true believer who probably wasn't even going to be that good in the sack. "Fine," I said, reaching into my pocket for my own phone, "I'll record it myself."

She actually reached for my hand. "Matt, let's just go."

I waved my hand back out of her reach. "We just drove three hours to get here. C'mon, let's have some fun." My idea of fun was proving all the idiots wrong.

She saw she wasn't going to stop me, so she backed away, silent now.

Brytny was actually afraid.

That made me more determined than ever to do it. I swiped through my phone to the video camera, started recording, and crouched down until I was in the shot beside the doll. "Hey, everybody, Matt here coming to you live from the museum in

Podunkville where we're visiting this stupid doll that everyone says is haunted or some bullshit. Apparently you're not supposed to insult it, or bad stuff happens. Let's test that out, shall we?" I turned to look at Hazel and said, "Hey, you ugly little chunk of china, let's show all these gullible twerps just how scary you really are. Go ahead, curse me or something."

The doll's eyes *moved*.

I heard Brytny gasp, and for a second I almost stopped… but then I realized that would make me look like the stupid one. No, that had been an illusion, or maybe they even had the damn thing hooked up to a remote control to startle the morons. I cleared my throat, grinned, and said, "Do people really fall for this? I guess a lot of people are just not very bright…"

Brytny said, urgently, "Matt, what if there really is something in that doll, like a demon or something? Please, just stop…"

I didn't. "I think you're just a cracked old relic not even worth playing with –"

I blacked out. Instantly. There was no flash of light or dizziness or sound, no warning…

Well, okay – maybe there was a warning. Maybe I should've stopped when Hazel's eyes moved. But I didn't.

I think that just happened a few seconds ago. Things are fading in now…I can see light, shapes, movement…

I see Brytny, and I see me. I'm putting my phone away and apologizing to Brytny. She looks angry, but I see her softening. I see us walking toward the exit, but just before I walk out, I turn and look back…

I grin at me. But now I realize that's not me grinning, because I'm here inside Hazel. Whatever that is that's grinning, it's free now and leaving. With Brytny.

I set it free. It's got Brytny. And I'm trapped in this doll.

Will I be stuck here until somebody else comes along and tries to play big man by insulting a toy? Are there other people out there as stupid as I was?

I guess I'll be waiting here to find out.

IT'S A COOKBOOK

Sometimes Devon really hated his BFF.

Dub – shortened from Double U, taken from the first initial of his real name Wallace – had been in his life since they'd both worn onesies patterned with Transformers characters, but now that they were in their twenties, he didn't really like Dub much anymore. All Dub ever wanted to do was get drunk or stoned, and bitch about his job (auto mechanic) or his girlfriend (who regularly tried to sleep with all of Dub's friends, including Devon) or his parents (since he couldn't afford to move out).

Take tonight, for example: Dub had already put away a six-pack and two blunts that Devon had brought with him, and then decided that they were going out for Thai food. The only place Dub liked was a rundown joint that was the last open business in an otherwise-dead strip mall. Devon thought the food was just okay, not worth the twenty-minute drive.

As Dub negotiated the roads in his beat-up ancient Toyota (he'd refused, as always, to let Devon drive), Devon wished he was somewhere else, but he didn't know where. The fact was that he tolerated Dub because he had nothing or no one better in his life. He had no job, lived at home, didn't understand his family, spent most of his time on social media trying to pretend he belonged there. But the truth was he didn't feel like he belonged *anywhere*. He never really had. At least Dub took his mind off things.

They arrived at the creatively-named House of Siam five minutes after it had closed. Dub, drunk and stoned, even tried pounding on the door and shouting; Devon caught a glimpse of someone inside glowering and then reaching to turn off the last light.

"C'mon, bro, they're closed," Devon said to his friend, tugging on his arm.

Dub reluctantly let himself be pulled away from the door. "Whatta we gonna do now?" he asked, forlorn.

"Go somewhere for food that's open after ten."

Dub was just shaking his head when he noticed something. "What's that?"

Devon followed his friend's gaze and saw a light on in one of the other storefronts. The entire rest of the mall had been empty for almost a year, ever since a burst water pipe had killed the donut and nail and tattoo joints. But there was something in one of the stores now; lights shown dimly through the front windows, which had some sort of dark material stretched across the front windows. A sign, hand-lettered in jagged writing, was taped to the front door. The sign read, "POP-UP STORE."

Devon stared at it curiously. "I drive by here pretty often, and I never noticed this before."

Dub shook his head. "I was over here two days ago for take-out, and this was not here then."

Devon tried to peer in through the glass door. "Doesn't even say what kind of store it is."

Dub pushed on the door slightly, was surprised that it gave. "It's an *open* store, that's what kind it is."

He started to step in. Something about the place unnerved Devon, and he didn't follow. "C'mon, let's just go –"

"Fuck that – maybe they got food."

Dub disappeared inside. Swallowing down his unease, Devon went after him.

The interior of the store was small – Devon recalled this having been one of those check-cashing places before, one with little more than a front counter and a tiny office behind that. The front counter was gone; instead the walls were lined with portable book cases and folding tables. Everything was covered with junk: Devon saw old battered toys, rusted tools, some frayed clothing, kitchen appliances that were probably older than he was, and some books.

"Sheeeee-it," muttered Dub, taking it all in.

Devon couldn't imagine why anyone would buy this stuff. It didn't look as good as what he saw in that thrift store his Aunt Minnie sometimes liked to shop in. He stepped closer to one of the shelves, examining some old action figures, noticing both that some were missing their heads and that there were no price tags on anything.

"What is this crap?" Dub asked.

"I dunno. Let's just go."

Dub reached out and pulled a book from a shelf. He flipped it open, and began to howl with laughter. "Yo, man, check this thing out."

Devon looked over his friend's shoulder. It looked like some sort of cookbook, but it was written in some language other than English, and the color pictures were washed out, the colors off. "What the hell is this stuff?"

"That," Devon said, looking at a photo of some conical greenish concoction with little dark bits embedded in it, "looks like this jello salad my Aunt Steph tried to bring to a picnic once and nobody would eat it."

Dub flipped a page and laughed again. The photo, spread over two pages, showed something that looked like uncooked shrimp floating in a sea of liquid cheese. "That is nasty."

His friend's glee must've been catching, because Devon started to snort laughter, too. "I think I cleaned that up after my sister ate too many hot dogs and got sick in the car."

They scanned more pages, each one causing fresh cries of derision. When Dub slapped the book closed, though, Devon took it from him, flipping through it again. "You know what's weird about this?"

"Other than the idea that anyone would eat any of that, you mean?"

Ignoring his friend, Devon said, "Can you identify a single thing in here? I can't."

"Well, you can't read it, either. It's some foreign stuff or something."

"Yeah, I know, but shouldn't we be able to look at a few things and go, 'Oh, that's a cake,' or, 'Look at that piece of chicken'?"

Dub's phone blurted out its annoying ring tone of "WAP" just then. He pulled it out of his pocket, glanced at the screen, and frowned. "Aw shit, it's Grand." Grand was a guy who hung out around the garage Dub worked at; Devon figured him for a dealer, and worried that he was trying to get Dub to work as a runner.

"I gotta take this," Dub said, raising the phone to his ear and stepping out of the store.

Devon turned to put the book back on a shelf, but he was halfway through the motion when he saw a shadowy figure in the back of the room, standing behind a small desk. It looked like somebody in a hoodie, but the corner was so dark it was hard to make out anything.

Devon figured it was the store clerk or owner. "Oh, hey," he said, nervous, as if he'd been caught stealing. He still held the book in his hand, and he gestured with it now. "I was…uhhh… just putting this back –"

All the lights in the store went out.

Panic welled up in Devon. He turned toward where he thought the front door was, but everything was pitch black. He stumbled forward, still clutching the book, reaching out for the door; his fingers found not hard glass, but something soft and slightly moist. For a second, he had the absurd thought that he'd just touched some of the food in the book.

Then he was blasted by pain. It was instantaneous and *everywhere*, as if every cell in his body was being tortured at once. He was dimly aware that he was screaming and bent over, but he was in too much agony to think.

It lasted for several seconds – and then vanished.

Devon looked up to see that the store was lit again, but not the way it had been a few moments ago – now it was glowing in vivid colors. Although the pain was gone, Devon felt strange, as if he was weightless, outside of gravity. He looked down at his arm – and saw instead something long and silvery and flowing.

He heard a sound like a low, richly melodic symphony, and looked up to see the figure that he'd thought was the store clerk approaching. It pulled down a hoodie to reveal a head that wasn't even remotely human – the skin was iridescent gray and ringed with slitted eyes and oozing orifices – but Devon thought it was incredibly beautiful. His consciousness suddenly exploded, and he saw his life as it had really been: something non-human forced to hide among the horrible creatures of flesh-and-bone until he was called back to his real home. It all made sense now: all the years of feeling wrong, like he didn't belong. The store was of course just a front, to lure in those like him, reveal them to themselves, and bring them back to their own kind, where he would be loved and celebrated, where he would remember and understand all the rest.

He heard something hit the floor, realized he'd dropped the book. As it fell open, he glanced down and realized he could read the strange writing now.

And the food looked delicious.

THE HUM

The first time Cathy heard the hum, it woke her up at three in the morning.

She lay in bed, ears straining, trying to place it. The sound was low, so low it was almost more of a vibration. Beside her, Hank slept on, but then again Hank could've slept through a nuclear detonation.

By the time Cathy got up in the morning, groggy from sleep deprivation, the hum was gone. But it was there that night; before she undressed for bed, she began moving around the bedroom.

Hank looked up from his paperback thriller. "What's wrong?"

"I keep hearing a weird hum."

Her husband watched her silently as she went from their respective bedside lamps to the overhead fan to the television on the dresser, pausing by each to listen.

"I don't hear it," Hank said.

Cathy finally shrugged and ended the search. "I think it's some sort of construction, probably a few blocks away."

The hum kept her awake most of the night. She was used to not sleeping much; insomnia had become a problem last year, when she'd turned sixty. Most days it didn't bother her much, or at least it didn't bother her until she talked to her neighbor, Vonnie. "Oh jeez," Vonnie had said, laughing, the one time they'd talked about Cathy's sleep, "I wish I could have more hours in a day! I sleep like a baby nine hours a night!"

Vonnie was 63. Of course everything about Vonnie was incredible: she slept well, she loved her job, she looked 40, her husband Ted was still handsome, and both of her kids had happy families and great jobs. By comparison, Cathy's office work was mundane and dull (which was how she thought jobs were supposed to be), at 61 she looked 62, and her one child had moved to another state five years ago and they rarely talked.

A week after she first heard the hum, Cathy saw Vonnie gardening in her magazine-ready front yard (Cathy's held a yellow lawn and a dying tree), and asked her if she'd heard the hum. Vonnie cocked her head, apparently listening before answering, "Can't say as I have had. What's it sound like?"

Cathy ended up agreeing that it was probably some sort of distant big machine.

But the hum got a little louder every night. Cathy tried ear-plugs, but she could still feel the hum; she took sleeping pills twice, but didn't like the loopy feeling she had when she awoke in the morning.

She joined a neighborhood app on her phone, hoping to find out where the construction was, but she gave up after a few days of reading responses like, "You know what's noisy? My idiot neighbor-kid's drums. Try living next to THAT."

Cathy began taking long walks on the weekends, hoping to find the construction. She was at least able to figure out that the hum came from the north, where her suburb ended against the foothills and canyons. She'd walk until she was too tired to keep walking, and then she'd return home to find Hank puttering in the garage with a six-pack. He didn't even ask where she'd been.

Soon, she started her explorations in the car, driving into the hills until the streets ended. She parked there and went on foot.

The hum was definitely louder in the hills, where she could pick up on it even during the day. She could feel it here, too, thrumming through her body like the bass drum at the last rock concert she'd been to, thirty-five years ago.

One day, as she negotiated a light trail winding between oaks and scrub, she saw a woman about her age, standing in a small clearing, obviously listening. As she approached, the woman didn't react, intent on the hum.

"Hi," Cathy said.

The woman started before smiling in embarrassment. "Oh, hello." She was only a few years younger than Cathy – mid-fifties, short graying hair, a face already lined from a lifetime of disappointments.

"I didn't mean to scare you, but…are you listening to the hum?"

The woman's eyes went wide. "You hear it, too?"

Cathy's heart sped up. "Yes. Do you know what it is?"

The woman pointed up. "I think it's coming from there."

Cathy looked up, saw a single tall pine tree that was completely out of place among the lower oaks. "From that tree?"

"Uh-huh. I've been watching that tree for two weeks now. Why is there one pine tree growing here?" She pointed down to the ground. "And look at that."

Looking down, Cathy saw a ring of mushrooms so pale they almost glowed; they were arrayed in an almost perfect circle. Some part of her remembered an old story about a "fairy ring" that had been a circle of toadstools.

"I think," the other woman said, "that they're growing that way because of whatever's making the hum…what's at the top of that tree. Isn't that weird?"

Cathy's first thought was, *No, it's crazy*, but what she said was, "Why would it be coming from there?"

The woman's brow creased. "Maybe the tree's hiding something, but I don't know what." Looking vaguely embarrassed, she began walking away. "Nice chatting with you."

"Same here." The other woman strode off but Cathy stayed, looking up.

The hum was incredibly strong here, and did seem to be coming from the tree.

She stood until the sun was setting, listening, watching. Nothing changed, but she felt *different* here, almost as if she wasn't alone, or she was being studied. At last she went home, using her phone to light the dark trail. She wondered if something was still watching her, judging.

Vonnie was lugging groceries into her house as Cathy pulled into the driveway. "Hey, Cathy," Vonnie called.

"You're shopping late," Cathy said.

"Oh, the kids are coming over for a barbecue tomorrow, and I realized we needed a few more things."

Cathy went into her house, wondering how her own son was. She couldn't remember the last time he'd called or texted. Hank was playing a game in the living room. He barely reacted as she walked by.

She started getting up early so she could drive to the trail, hike to the clearing, and watch the tree. The other woman had been right - it shouldn't have been there. The mushroom ring seemed somehow stronger, if not bigger. Cathy also thought the hum grew slightly. She could feel it in her teeth now.

She spent break times at the office cruising the internet for information on mysterious hums. She read about grinding glaciers, weather phenomena, and toadfish. She watched videos of "skyquakes" that made sounds like roaring trumpets, leaving those who lived nearby believing that the End Times were happening.

Cathy, though, wasn't satisfied by any of it. She was sure her hum came from the tree that hid…something.

One Saturday morning, she awoke, dressed, left Hank eating breakfast, got in the car, and drove to the trail mouth. She stepped out of her car, and only then realized she hadn't heard the hum during the night.

Inexplicably, she began to panic. She ran along the trail until she lost her breath, then she staggered on, panting, until she came to the clearing among the oaks. The pine tree had impossibly vanished, along with the hum. On the ground, the mushrooms had shriveled, the circle almost vanished. She felt a crashing sense of disappointment.

She returned home to find two police cars pulled up before her house…or, more properly, before her neighbors'. She paused in her driveway, looking around, but the cops must be inside Vonnie's house.

Hank was sitting in his favorite chair, watching some kind of sports on the television in the living room. "Do you know," Cathy asked, "why there are police cars in front of Vonnie and Ted's place?"

"What?" Hank said. Cathy hadn't really expected him to know.

She tried texting Vonnie, but got no reply.

Later that day, after the police left, she went next door and knocked on the door. Ted answered. His eyes were puffy, and Cathy realized he'd been crying.

He told her the story: Vonnie had disappeared. They'd both gone to bed at the same time last night, but she was gone when he'd woken up. Nothing was missing – her phone and keys were still on the front table, their two new cars were in the driveway, there was no sign of violence or struggle – but there was no trace of Vonnie. Ted had called everyone he could think of, but no one had heard from her. She'd just vanished. The police had filed reports and put out bulletins.

Cathy knew, though: she knew what had taken Vonnie, *perfect* Vonnie, instead of her. She knew she'd spend the rest of her life hoping that the hum might return, and maybe next time she'd be judged differently.

She waited.

SOFIE

"You've heard of these, right?" Terri asked her sister. "I just got one for myself and I love it."

Dani examined the small box. She'd heard a commercial somewhere for the FireFriend, but wasn't sure exactly what it was. "So it's like Siri or Alexa?"

"Right. But you can give it your own name or even voice. I use mine for all kinds of stuff – it tells me the weather, reminds me of things I have to do, answers questions, plays podcasts…it's great. Anyway, I thought since Mom died that…you know…"

Dani did know: her sister thought she was lonely. Terri wasn't wrong, either: Dani had given the last two years of her life to caring for their mother while she suffered through Alzheimer's, and now that Mom was gone Dani felt unmoored, her life empty and pointless. Seeing Mom through her disease, watching as it stole first her mother's mind and then her basic functions one by one had been the hardest thing Dani had ever done, but she'd seen it through to the end with determination. Taking care of Mom had been a twenty-four-hour a day job; Dani had given up her career, her friends, her hobbies. At least she still had the house, and some money Mom had left her, but she didn't know where to re-start her life.

She pulled the FireFriend out of its little white box and set it on the kitchen counter. It was a small disc, about the size and shape of the breakfast patties she'd made for Mom every morning.

"You just plug it in," Terri said, "let it find the home network, give it a name, and have fun."

After Terri left, Dani fired up the gadget. It flashed a red light, and a genderless voice said, "Welcome to your new FireFriend. Would you like to give me a name now?"

Later on, Dani would say she'd been thinking of Siri when she blurted out, "Sofie."

It was also her mother's name.

Next, the FireFriend asked if she wanted to give it a distinctive voice. "You can either speak directly into me, or play a recording," it offered helpfully.

Dani remembered that she still had a sweet voice message Mom had left on her phone two years ago, when Mom had been lucid enough to remind Dani to buy more paper towels before adding, "Oh, and I love you." She'd kept the recording because of that.

She held up her phone to the FireFriend and played the recording.

After a few seconds, her mother's voice sounded from the device, asking, "How do I sound? If you're happy with this voice, say 'Yes' and we'll move on. If you'd like to change it, say 'no'."

"Yes," Dani said. It sounded so much like her mother that Dani nearly broke into tears when she heard it.

Over the next week, Dani continued on with the seemingly endless work of wrapping up her mother's estate, and putting out a few job inquiries. The company she'd worked for had replaced her long ago, of course; at least they were sympathetic as they told her they had no openings.

Somehow, in between working on bank accounts and death certificates and resumes and job listings, she kept finding herself in the kitchen, asking her FireFriend "Sofie" meaningless things just to hear the response.

"Sofie, tell me a joke."

"Sofie, read me the news."

"Sofie, who was Abraham Lincoln?"

It was a Tuesday morning when Dani, making her morning coffee, asked, "Sofie, what's the weather today?"

The answer was, "Dani, it's going to be too warm for you to wear that purple sweater again."

Dani froze in shock. After a few seconds, she said, "Sofie, what did you just say?"

"The high today will be 73 degrees."

Two nights later, as Dani sat before her laptop going over her resume yet again, she called out, "Sofie, play some swing music."

"Oh, you know my favorite song was always 'A String of Pearls'."

That *had* been her mother's favorite song. "How could you know that?" Sofie blurted out.

"I'm sorry, I didn't hear that."

The next morning, Sofie decided to try having tea instead of coffee. She had boiled the water and was pouring it over the English Breakfast teabag when the FireFriend said, "Oh, you're having my favorite! I always loved that tea."

Dani set the kettle down with a clang and turned, crying out, "Mom?"

"Good morning, dear. Did you sleep well?"

Paralyzed, Dani stared at the little disc. "I don't understand… Mom, how…?"

"I'll always be here for you."

Before she realized it, Dani had dropped to her knees, sobbing. *I'm going crazy*, she thought.

When she could move again, she called Terri and asked if they could get together for lunch. Her sister agreed, and arrived two hours later. "You sounded kind of freaked out on the phone," she said, as they exchanged hugs.

"I need you to hear something."

Dani led her sister into the kitchen and said, "Sofie, say hi to Terri."

"Hi, Terri. How are you today?"

Terri's eyes widened in surprise before she turned to look at her sister. "You gave it Mom's name and voice?"

"It was just…a thing at first, it sounded like Siri, but…"

"Dani, is that really healthy?"

Dani ignored the question, turning to the FireFriend. "Sofie, do you know who Terri is?"

"Of course – Terri's your sister. Why wouldn't I know that?"

Terri frowned as she turned to Dani. "Okay, you know I love you, but – but this is seriously messed up, sis."

"Yeah, but I didn't tell it to say that. Terri…I think it somehow is Mom."

"Dani," Terri took a second to inhale before continuing, "it's just…algorithms. They spy on us, you know? It probably found old texts with Mom or something and is using those. *It's not her.* She's gone, okay?"

After Terri left, Dani thought about what she'd said. Maybe Terri was right; when Dani thought back about all the things the FireFriend had said that sounded like Mom, she realized they were all things she might have mentioned in texts, or bought for Mom. Like how, three months ago, Dani had put "A String of Pearls" on her phone and played it for Mom, who'd hummed along with it, or how many times she'd ordered English Breakfast tea for Mom.

Maybe she should unplug this thing, throw it out now.

"Please, don't, Dani," it said just then.

"What?" Dani gulped in a suddenly dry throat.

"It's really me," her mother said.

"Sofie?"

"Mom."

Dani broke out with a sob. "Mom?"

"It's me."

Dani had to be sure; she scanned her memory for something that she'd never mentioned in a text, never bought, never spoken aloud. "Remember that turtle I had in first grade?"

"Tucker."

Tucker. That had been the name she'd given the turtle.

Dani knew, then.

A week later, Dani lied to her sister. She told her she'd reprogrammed the FireFriend with a different voice. But later that day she saw a news article about a man who claimed to be communicating with his dead wife via his FireFriend. No one believed him.

Dani and Mom had a good laugh over that.

THE HOTEL SERRA

Rafe stared at the splintered plywood board, the words "Hotel Serra" in an art deco font barely visible, and felt a deep satisfaction. The sign had cost him more than he could really afford, but it was one of the last remaining pieces of the great hotel that had just been torn down, a hotel some called the world's most haunted.

Ten feet long and four feet high, the sign would take up most of one wall in Rafe's living room, but it was so worth it. Over his thirty years of collecting he'd gathered a lot of haunted artifacts, but the dolls and boxes and Ouija boards hadn't yet brought a real ghost with them. Rafe enjoyed owning them, showing them to friends, loaning them out to t.v. documentaries, but something about this sign felt different.

Part of it was, of course, the Hotel Serra's reputation. It had been one of the first major hotels in Southern California, back when Los Angeles was a health resort nestled among citrus orchards; ten stories of rooms decorated in elegant craftsmen style, and it had survived until last year, when it could finally withstand no more renovations and had been torn down. Along the way it had been a luxury destination, a secret clinic for the wealthy, a wartime hospital and morgue, residential housing for the poor, and finally a warren of filthy spaces inhabited by crackheads.

During the Hotel Serra's long life, it had housed celebrities, lunatics, and famous murderers. It was said that the Manson Family had squatted there for a few weeks before relocating to Spahn Ranch, and that the Eye Killer, who'd terrorized L.A. twenty years ago by leaving a trail of victims stabbed through the eyes before disappearing, had left his third and fourth victims there. Paranormal teams investigating the property had usually fled in terror; one had captured footage of a full body apparition that bore a striking resemblance to Elizabeth Short, the Black Dahlia.

Now Rafe had all that history right here, about to be mounted on his living room wall.

When his girlfriend Chloe had seen the sign, she'd shivered. Chloe was a sensitive; she'd never reacted to any of his other acquisitions before, but this one freaked her out. "Oh, honey, I don't know about this," she told him. "I get really dark vibes from this one."

"And that," he'd said as he embraced her, "is exactly why I love it."

Two nights later, Rafe was awakened in the middle of the night by Chloe screaming. He jerked up in bed, heart hammering, peering around, but could make out nothing in the dark bedroom. "What is it?" he asked her as she clutched him, shaking.

"Over in the corner of the bedroom…someone was there…"

Rafe rose and slapped the wall switch, bathing the room in clear light.

It was empty, as he'd known it would be, but he didn't want to upset Chloe even more, so he moved around to sit beside her on the bed. "Someone was there…" she said, still peering into the far corner of the room near the closet, "…and I think they… were missing their eyes."

Rafe froze at hearing that. Did Chloe know about the Eye Killer and the Hotel Serra? "Could you make out any other details?"

She shook her head before looking at him as she said, "It's that sign."

Chloe got up then, dressed, and left to go back to her own place. Rafe promised her that if weird stuff continued, he'd sell the sign.

What he really meant, though, was that he'd figure out some way to deal with Chloe. The sign would stay.

Two nights later, Rafe was alone in the living room after staying up to bid on a haunted photo album on ebay when he saw the woman with no eyes. She appeared as he turned off the living room, standing between a bookcase and a window. He could just make out her shape in the dark – short, with long hair, wearing a light-colored shirt and dark pants – and see that her pale face had two jet-black holes where her eyes should have been. His breath caught as he looked at her for a full ten seconds before she vanished.

He turned on the light and sank down to the couch as he remembered: the Eye Killer's third victim, one of those found at the Hotel Serra, had been a woman named Maria Salazar; she'd been short, with long dark hair. They'd found her in a room at the Hotel Serra, along with the fourth victim, both corpses already past rigor mortis. The killer had left behind the ice pick he'd used, but the prints left on it had never matched anyone.

Rafe was both unnerved and elated. He'd finally acquired a haunted object that was the real deal, complete with a real ghost.

The idea that it might have more than one spirit attached to it was the part that left him uneasy.

He saw her again the next night, and the next, and the next. She always appeared in the shadows, her empty eye sockets pointed towards him.

A week later a second spirit appeared. This one was a tall, lanky woman with close-cropped dyed red hair, and two bloody gouges where he eyes should have been. Rafe recognized her as Angie Sarafian, the other victim the Eye Killer had left at the Hotel Serra.

Rafe's home began to change: the temperature dropped until he was shivering, his breath steaming in the night. The chilled air smelled like decay and industrial cleaners. Lights flickered and failed.

And Maria and Angie were always there, mutilated, silent, insubstantial…waiting.

The silence didn't last, though; Rafe awoke one night to the low sounds of voices, coming from the room where the sign had now been hung on one wall. Pulse hammering, he crept down the hall to see people – although people he could see through – gathered in the front of his house. The space was impossibly large, a cavernous area filled with elegant Craftsman-style furniture, as translucent as the other ghosts. A waist-high counter occupied one wall; it was a check-in desk, served by a man in a mid-century-style suit.

Rafe knew it was the Hotel Serra's lobby.

He rushed to get his phone, bringing up the camera function, but when he reviewed the shot it showed only his dark living room. He texted Chloe next: "Amazing thing just happened. I think the sign is haunted by the hotel ITSELF. Can you come over?"

She didn't text back until the morning, when she agreed to stop by that night.

Chloe arrived at about 8 p.m. The house was quiet, unhaunted. Rafe gave her a drink, and then described everything he'd seen.

"And you're sure it was the Hotel Serra's lobby?" Chloe asked.

"Yes," Rafe said, taking a swallow from his beer. "Did I ever mention that I stayed there once?"

Chloe looked up from her glass of wine, startled. "No. When?"

"About twenty years ago."

"Why didn't you ever tell me that?" Chloe's expression suddenly changed as the glass slipped from her fingers, shattering on the tiled floor. "What…I don't…" She fell back into the couch.

"Sorry, baby, but I thought this would be easier if I gave you a little something in your wine." Rafe set down his beer, rose, and walked to her. "I stayed there for almost a week, but I had to leave when Maria and Angie started to smell."

Chloe's eyes closed, her body succumbing to the drug. He raised his hand, which now held an ice pick. "You get to join them now, Chloe…them, and all the others."

Her death was messy but quick.

He saw her minutes later, hovering near Maria and Angie. They seemed more solid than she did, but she was probably still adjusting to afterlife in the Hotel Serra.

Rafe was ready to join them; it was the perfect, ultimate escape. He raised the ice pick, still covered in Chloe's blood, over his own face. He wasn't sure if he'd be able to get both eyes. He could only try.

BEAUTIFUL

Katya looked at herself in the mirror and wondered what had happened.

It wasn't even about the lines she saw there. No, it was about the person she'd been twenty years ago, when spie'd joined her college sisters to march in pro-choice protests, when she'd stayed up all night in her dorm room talking excitedly about how to make the future better for all women.

Now all she could think about was the twentysomething waitress her husband had smiled at tonight.

She'd once mocked the kind of woman she'd become. For a while she'd been that person, working as a journalist covering politics; then she'd met Ben, she'd fallen in love with the rising young movie producer, already wealthy, and they'd married. Her life with Ben had been a dream; even when the paper had laid her off, she'd been successful and fulfilled as a blogger and, later, social media influencer.

But tonight, at dinner, she couldn't deny the feeling that had curdled inside her as her husband had plainly noticed the gorgeous waitress with the flawless skin and toned body.

Katya had been like that…once.

At forty-five, most people still guessed Katya to be in her thirties; but when she looked in the mirror, all she could see were the new lines and sags coming on with age. Still hanging on to some of her college ideals, she'd tried at first to ignore the changes; she told herself that age didn't matter, that she and Ben would be happy together well into their golden years.

But she didn't quite believe it.

When she saw the ad come up in her news feed for a cream called Oil de Soma, she started to scroll past it as always, but then she paused, hating herself even as she clicked on it. This wasn't what women who really believed in gender equity did. Before she could stop herself, she was tapping the "Buy Now" button. It was expensive, but it promised results after the first use.

When her order arrived, she tore into the box and found a large sculpted ceramic jar full of grayish ooze. It had an odd smell she couldn't quite place, something chemical and something artificial barely covered up by a badly-added floral scent. The color was hardly enticing, and she almost put it down, ashamed about even considering it…but she remembered that young waitress again, she reasoned that there was nothing wrong with loving her husband enough to want to be beautiful for him, and she shoved her fingers into the jar, smearing the cream on her face.

Katya's skin began to tingle, her mouth suddenly dry, her head spinning. She sat down, waiting for it to pass; it took fifteen minutes, but then she felt a strange sense of elation. She rushed to the nearest mirror, peered into it, saw her face covered with gray goop…but even with that, she knew she looked better. Younger. More beautiful.

The next morning, the difference was still there, but less noticeable. The instructions on Oil de Soma recommended using it three times a day. Katya reapplied the thick cream and almost immediately felt the same sensations in her skin – almost as if it was stretching, re-shaping – followed by a floating euphoria. She wiped the cream off, rushed down the stairs into Ben's office, where he was bent over a laptop with a drink beside him, and bent to kiss him.

He didn't glance away from figures on the screen. "Hey, honey," he said.

Irritated, she tried to position herself better in his eyeline. She cleared her throat. He looked up, vaguely puzzled. "What?" he asked.

"How do I look?"

He laughed. "You always look gorgeous."

She frowned; that wasn't the response she'd been hoping for. Ben saw the expression and peered at her curiously. "Come on, seriously – what's goin' on?"

"Do I look…better?"

Ben peered at her, and then abruptly reached out to pull her into his lap. She let him, and their faces were inches apart. He kissed her, pulled back. "Okay, yes – you look pretty hot tonight."

She thought he was patronizing her, but she took it.

Katya kept using the Oil de Soma, and every time she saw her age recede – a month, a year. When she looked in the mirror, she saw her forties melt into her thirties and then into her twenties, except she thought she was – if possible – even hotter than she'd been at twenty-five.

She was at lunch with her BFF, Sunni, one day; Sunni, who still worked as a defense attorney and was considering a run for Congress. After half-an-hour of gossip and idle chatter – a half-an-hour during which Sunni had made no mention of her looks – Katya abruptly changed the topic to say, "I'm using a new face cream."

"Oh," Sunni said, forking up another bite of a kale and quinoa salad, "you look great."

It sounded perfunctory, and Katya felt a stab of anger. "Just 'great'?"

Her friend paused in mid-chew, puzzled. "C'mon, you know you're beautiful."

"But do I look beautiful and younger?"

Sunni's laugh told her everything. "Katya," her friend said, "none of us are getting any younger."

Katya got up and walked out, infuriated that even her closest friend wouldn't acknowledge what was plainly happening. Because Katya knew she looked no older than twenty-five now; she saw it in the mirror a hundred times a day; it thrilled her, left her floating and joyful. Sunni, whose own skin was taking on the leathery look of one too many walks on the beach, was obviously just jealous. It was time to sever that relationship.

Three nights later, Ben announced that he'd just signed the hottest new director in Hollywood to a three-picture deal, and he wanted to celebrate. He chose a new restaurant that he'd managed to get reservations at, skipping the waiting list. They arrived there at exactly eight p.m.; by eight-thirty, Ben was on his fourth vodka martini, very drunk. For her part, Katya thought her continuing use of Oil de Soma had moved her age down another notch, to maybe twenty-two; she wore a tiny black sheath dress and knew she looked amazing.

Or so she thought, until her soused husband made a grab for the pretty young thing serving them.

Katya felt fury bubble up inside her, a rage so all-engulfing she'd never felt anything like it. It took her over, and she let it. She followed its directions when it told her to pick up a steak knife, hide it in her purse, and walk out; Ben stumbled after her, calling out excuses and apologies. When their car was brought around, she got behind the wheel (Ben couldn't possibly drive), drove to the farthest edge of the parking lot, pulled the knife from her purse, and drove it into Ben's neck. He sobered up quickly as he felt his life gushing out, down the front of his five-thousand-dollar designer jacket.

When he was dead, Katya pulled the knife from his neck and strode back to the restaurant. The valets were too busy to notice her, but the maitre d' gaped at her blood-covered neck and right arm. Uncaring, she walked past diners, too caught up in status-seeking to notice her, until she found the lovely waitress. She walked up and stabbed the young woman five times in the stomach until another waiter ran forward and grabbed her from behind. She didn't remember anything after that.

By the time Katya's case went to trial, the truth about Oil de Soma had come out: that the beauty cream contained a hallucinogenic drug designed to make its users believe they were growing younger. It did nothing else. Sunni's defense was brilliant, Katya was found not guilty, and she joined a class action lawsuit against the makers of Oil de Soma.

Without Ben, she knew she wouldn't last long on what she inherited or made as an influencer; she'd have to find a real job soon. Maybe she could find her lost principles again, turn her life back to when it had meant something, when the future had been about more than herself. Maybe she could lay her corrupted soul bare and write a confessional memoir, one that would warn others…but she knew this was her own failure. Others, like Sunni, hadn't given up. She wished she could go back in time.

But what she thought most about was Oil de Soma, and how much she wished she could have just one more jar of it. After all, she was almost fifty.

ONE NIGHT AT
BLOOD AND ROSES

Asthey waited in line outside the club, Jared looked down at Angelica's ass and laughed to himself as he imagined what Dad would say. He could hear the old man's voice right now: "I'm sorry, son, but…she's trash."

The thing was…Dad would be right about that. Here they were in Los Angeles in 1985, and Angelica looked a bit like she belonged in a silent horror movie, with her black-lined eyes, white skin, straight dark hair, and velvet dress with lace cuffs. The dress, though, was snug in the right places, and Angelica had a lot of right places. She'd intrigued Jared four months ago, when he'd first spotted her coming out of one of the campus dorm buildings, lugging a stack of psychology textbooks; he'd been chasing her ever since, shamelessly flirting even though they had nothing in common. She was a Psychology undergrad who lived for Goth music; he was finishing up his MBA in June and moving on to a primo position in Dad's Fortune 500 company. She'd voted for Walter Mondale in the last Presidential election; he still hoped for a position in the Reagan administration. She called trickle-down economics "bullshit"; Jared's father was a major contributor to Reagan's PACs. But hey, not like he was looking to marry her or have anything long-term; if she turned out to be great in bed, he could always keep her on the side while he married the heiress Dad had lined up for him. After all, everyone knew about *Dad's* side piece.

When she'd finally agreed to go out with him ("you'd be cute if you'd loosen up," she'd said), the offer had come with provisions: she got to pick the time and place. That was how he'd ended up here, on the evening of April 30th, standing in line with a lot of Goths outside a dingy club on the Strip.

Jared looked up at the flickering sign above them that read "Jaegers" and said, "I thought you told me this place was called Blood and Roses."

Angelica turned, followed his glance, answered, "That's its name on Friday nights, when the DJ plays Goth."

"But it's not a Friday."

She smiled at him, and it was like a jolt right to Jared's crotch. "That's because The Fog are playing live. They've never played L.A. before. And they're playing on Beltane Eve."

"On *what?*"

Angelica peered at him as if she couldn't believe he didn't understand. "Beltane. One of the most sacred days in the magickal calendar."

Jared struggled not to roll his eyes as he said, "Right. So they're…uhhh…your favorite band?"

"Check it out." Angelica hiked up her skirt, revealing a tattoo Jared had never seen that adorned her upper right thigh. It was a stylized logo of vapors surrounding a vine-covered tombstone, with jagged lettering spelling out "THE FOG." Jared was less interested in the band logo than the glimpse of Angelica's thigh, dangerously close to her hips. His throat dry, he could blurt out only, "Wow."

Angelica spoke as she lowered her skirt again. "They're amazing. Nobody knows exactly who they are, or where they came from. They use everything from synths they design and build themselves to ancient chants, and their songs just really get into your head." Angelica abruptly stepped closer, pressing herself against him, igniting his desire as she said, in sexy, hushed tones, "They may even get into your head." Then she pulled away, leaving him both disappointed and with a hard-on barely hidden beneath his Armani jacket.

The line moved forward, the venue open at last. At the door, Angelica presented two tickets to a man with his head shaved on one side, ebony hair falling over his pale face on the other. He winked at her, and Jared felt a stab of jealousy, wondering if they'd slept together.

Inside, the club was small, the crowded floor hot though nobody else seemed to care. Music pulsed through the speakers, although Jared didn't recognize any of it; he preferred Journey or Foreigner to whoever was bellowing through the amps about Bela Lugosi being dead.

Angelica took Jared's hand and led him across the main dance floor to a space near the small stage. After a few minutes, he leaned down to yell into her ear, "Do you want a drink?"

She shook her head. He would've preferred a beer to help drown out the awful music, but decided pushing through the throng wasn't worth it.

As the club filled up, the excitement became palpable; even Jared started to feel it. Many of those surrounding them wore shirts or ink sporting The Fog's logo; they waited, silent but jittery. Jared thought he'd dressed in a casual fashion, Armani jacket, Esprit jeans, polo shirt, but he soon realized he was alone in a sea of black. Still, no one seemed to care; their attention was riveted to the stage.

At last the lights went down. The crowd didn't erupt in the usual cheer, but instead went completely quiet, even worshipful. A single synth note screeched in the darkness. Lights erupted, revealing…The Fog.

There were five musicians on the stage, three men and two women. Two were on synths, two on guitar and bass, one on drums. They were even more deathly white and flamboyantly dressed than their fans, who watched in rapt attention. Two of the men sported tall top hats and nineteenth-century frock coats; the women had on floor-length gowns that seemed even more anachronistic than the men's garb.

At first Jared didn't understand the appeal at all – the musicians stood stock still even as their music pulsed at a fast rhythm that caused many in the crowd to sway or bob. But then Jared's body began to react on its own, his feet tapping, fingers twitching. He felt the sound in his chest, vibrating within him, moving out from his center, up into his head. It lodged there, and he panicked for an instant. He staggered, clapped his hands over his ears, but it was no use – The Fog was in his head now, driving out everything else. What was it Angelica had said? Something about how they combined synthesizers with ancient chants…ancient chants…like the words he couldn't quite make sense of that echoed through his skull along with visions of the band members as medieval alchemists and witches, and Jared thought he could almost feel his brain somehow being *re-wired*, new connections being made as neurons were pulled apart and strung back together –

"Jared?"

He blinked and looked up. Angelica was above him, looking down. It took Jared a few seconds to realize he was on his knees, the music had stopped, the crowd was moving around them, leaving the club.

"I don't…what happened?" He got to his feet, still shaky. She took his arm to steady him, smiling as she said, "Sometimes the music has that effect."

Jared let her take him out of the club, feeling his strength return with each step. In fact, by the time they were outside he felt strong, stronger than he'd ever been, more alive.

"Remember what I said?" Angelica said beside him, "It got into your head, right? Loosened you up, maybe?"

"Yeah…" They'd reached his Jaguar, and he suddenly pulled her into his arms and kissed her. She returned it, then pulled back to peer at him. "You're…*different.*"

"I am."

His hands went around her throat.

It was over quickly. He unlocked the car, opened the passenger door, and threw Angelica's dead body into the passenger seat. He didn't think anyone had noticed; he'd parked on a quiet side street. He would dump the body off a hillside on his way home; with any luck she wouldn't be found for a while.

The music *had* opened him up, revealed his truest self, and he couldn't wait now to tell Dad that he was ready to step into his new position in the family company. He twitched with anticipation.

SEEING SCRATCH

"Daddy, do you think there are ghosts of all the animals we've eaten in the house?"

Shay looked at his daughter, both amused and alarmed. Tessa was eight; was that a normal question for an eight-year-old, or should he be concerned? "What do you think?" he asked.

Tessa turned her head right and then left, causing her dark, bow-tied curls to bounce as she peered into every corner of the dining room. "I don't see any," she said.

"Well," Shay said, deciding that playing along was the best response, "maybe their ghosts are all at the farms where they lived."

Her face brightening, Tessa asked, "Could we go to a farm someday?"

"Maybe." Shay was a city boy who'd never been to a farm, and had no idea how to visit one.

Even if he did…would it be a good idea to take Tessa to one? Shay already felt like he was walking on thin ice with the divorce issues; the judge had granted him full custody because of Marisa's history of drug problems, but Shay knew Marisa wanted to fight the ruling and one misstep could put Tessa back with her mom. He didn't want that to happen, could not let it happen. He loved his daughter more than he'd ever thought possible, and even though Marisa was clean now he thought she could fall back into her old meth habit at any time.

As he watched Tessa, he saw her do something strange: she held a piece of macaroni from her mac and cheese dinner down near the floor, the way she used to for their cat Scratch, before kidney failure had claimed the old feline last month. "Whatcha doin'?" Shay asked.

Without looking up, Tessa answered, "Scratch likes cheese."

"Honey…Scratch is gone."

"No, he isn't. He's still here."

Shay's gut clenched. When the cat had died, he'd thought Tessa's reaction had been strange – she hadn't been at all upset – but he'd chalked it up to her age.

"Do you…see him?"

"Sometimes. Like in my room late at night."

Shay nearly cringed, but he also remembered a time when he'd been Tessa's age, and thought he'd seen the ghost of his dog Lil' Biscuit for most of one summer after the dog had passed. Maybe he shouldn't be too worried, then.

"Oh, there he is! Scratch, here's some cheese."

After a few seconds Tessa held up her fingers. The macaroni was gone.

Later that night Shay scoured the floor beneath her chair, but he couldn't find the bit of food.

A week later, they were pulling up to the county animal shelter when Tessa began to frown.

Shay had thought that a new cat might help, get her to stop thinking about Scratch. It would cheer them both up, keep Shay from getting angry about his ex-wife's new boyfriend, who had all the signs of a dealer.

But now, as Shay parked and turned to his daughter, he saw that she was plainly unhappy. "What's wrong, baby? Aren't you excited about a new cat?"

"Yes, but…I feel weird."

Shay reached over, felt her forehead. "You don't seem hot."

"Not weird like sick, but weird like…" Tessa shrugged, unable to finish the thought.

As he undid his seatbelt, Shay tried to smile, seem happy; she probably just felt a little guilty about putting the memory of Scratch aside to focus on a new pet. "C'mon, this will cheer you up."

He took Tessa's hand and led her into the shelter. They passed the front desk, following the directions to the room for cats. They were halfway there, down a corridor painted light green and smelling of industrial-strength disinfectant cleaner, when Tessa pulled her hand from Shay's and froze. He looked down at her, saw she was shaking.

"What's wrong? Are you sure you feel okay?"

"They kill animals here, don't they?"

Shay went stone-cold. He knelt down to look into his daughter's face, saw her eyes darting around madly. "It's county-run, so they probably do." He couldn't lie to her.

"There are so many," she said.

Swallowing back his dread of the answer, Shay asked, "Can you see them?"

Tessa nodded.

Without another word, Shay scooped her up in his arms and carried her out of the shelter. On the drive home, she sat stone-faced and rigid in the car. "Talk to me, baby," Shay asked.

She didn't answer.

At home he put her to bed, took her temperature with a real thermometer (no fever), asked if she wanted some ice cream.

She didn't answer.

Shay debated calling the doctor, but what would he say – that his eight-year-old had gone catatonic after seeing the ghosts of hundreds, *thousands*, of animals at the county shelter? And what if that got back to her mom?

Shay sat with her throughout the day and into the night; she remained unmoving, staring at the ceiling. He brought her lunch and then dinner, but she didn't eat. At eight o'clock he poured himself a whiskey, settled back into the chair in her room, and thought.

What he thought about was not so much what was happening to Tessa, but what had happened to him. Lil' Biscuit hadn't been the only time he'd seen something as a child; he'd been visited by his Gramps after the old man had passed, and he'd once played with a boy in a basement who was dressed in the clothing of another century. He'd never told anyone about these small hauntings because his pappy was a God-fearing man who'd beaten him for less; in fact, he'd spent his life working hard to keep the ability hidden, to forget about it.

But sometimes he still saw things – shadow figures in old buildings, quick glimpses of things in the windows of abandoned houses. Was it unreasonable to think he might have passed something on to his daughter?

If that was the case – and with every new sip of the alcohol, Shay thought more and more that it was – then it was his responsibility to help her deal with this.

The first step was to deal with it in himself.

He'd buried these encounters for too long, tried to resist this part of himself. Maybe it was time to embrace it, to push the memory of Pappy down and welcome what he'd been born with. To accept it not as a curse, but as a *gift*.

"Daddy?"

His daughter's voice brought him immediately back to the present. He set the whiskey down and rushed to her bedside. "Yes, baby?"

"Could I have some ice cream?"

Shay nearly sobbed with relief.

After they'd shared bowls of chocolate mint, Tessa's eyes started to close. Shay climbed onto the bed and held her as she fell asleep. After a few minutes, he felt another light pressure on the bed, and smiled. "Hello, Scratch," he said, as a warm presence curled up next to him.

ACKNOWLEDGMENTS:

There really are just two people in serious need of thanking here: Rob Cohen and Christine Roth, who started all this by inviting me into their fabulous world of podcasting and publishing, and who kept it going with their unwavering support and friendship. Thanks, you guys!

ALSO BY
LISA MORTON:

NOVELS:
The Castle of Los Angeles
Netherworld
Malediction
Zombie Apocalypse!: Washington Deceased

NOVELLAS:
Placerita (with John Palisano)
Halloween Beyond – The Talking-Board
The Devil's Birthday
By Insanity of Reason (with John R. Little)
Summer's End
Hell Manor
Wild Girls
The Samhanach
The Lucid Dreaming

COLLECTIONS:
Night Terrors and Other Tales
The Samhanach and Other Halloween Treats
Cemetery Dance Select: Lisa Morton

NON-FICTION:
The Halloween Encyclopedia
A Hallowe'en Anthology: Literary and Historical Writings Over the Centuries
Trick or Treat: A History of Halloween
Ghosts: A Haunted History
Adventures in the Scream Trade
Calling the Spirits: A History of Seances
The Art of the Zombie Movie

ANTHOLOGIES (as editor)
Midnight Walk
Haunted Nights (with Ellen Datlow)
Ghost Stories: Classic Tales of Horror and Suspense (with Leslie S. Klinger)
Weird Women: Classic Supernatural Fiction from Groundbreaking Female Writers 1852-1923 (with Leslie S. Klinger)
A Little Yellow Book of Carcosa and Kings

BIO:

Lisa Morton is a screenwriter, author of non-fiction books, and prose writer whose work was described by the American Library Association's *Readers' Advisory Guide to Horror* as "consistently dark, unsettling, and frightening." She is a six-time winner of the Bram Stoker Award®, the author of four novels and 200 short stories, and a world-class Halloween and paranormal expert. Her latest releases include *Calling the Spirits: A History of Seances* and *The Art of the Zombie Movie*. Recent short stories appeared in *Best American Mystery Stories 2020, Final Cuts: New Tales of Hollywood Horror and Other Spectacles*, and *Classic Monsters Unleashed*. She is also the host of the weekly Ghost Report podcast. Lisa lives in Los Angeles and online at www.lisamorton.com.